The Gentle Tourist

The Gentle Tourist

a novel by
JILL DELAY

ANDRE DEUTSCH

First published 1986 by
André Deutsch Limited
105 Great Russell Street London WC1B 3LJ

Copyright © 1986 by Jill Delay

All rights reserved

ISBN 233 97872 0

Phototypeset by AKM Associates (UK) Ltd
Ajmal House, Hayes Road, Southall, London
Printed in Great Britain by
Ebenezer Baylis and Son Ltd, Worcester

Elisha took hold of his own clothes,
and rent them in two pieces.
He took up also the mantle of
Elijah that fell from him.

King II 12

Chapter 1

'Oh my God!' said the American girl outside the Palermo coffee bar. 'Just look at that, willya?' She had sat down at a table near the door and was holding a freckled leg up in the air. She waved the foot up and down. Most of the bottom layer of her ethnic sandal flapped about, torn away from the rest of the sole, and by the look of her she hadn't any other shoes. Her possessions were crammed into a tall rucksack of blue nylon on a slender aluminium frame.

From the bar just inside the door, several men were watching her silently. Lorenzo D'Ayala was among them, stirring his coffee with a well-manicured hand, and thinking. The men around him were short and stocky, dark, with troubled faces: they would have been amazed had they discovered the revolutionary thoughts in the mind of this tall, silver-haired man whose open face and pale eyes seemed to signal barely anything at all.

D'Ayala was thinking about his married life, his wife, Mariella, having recently died. Appalled, he saw behind him a wasteland where the pair of them had cultivated nothing but hollow dignity, privacy, and the perpetuation of small privileges of class. Appalled, but hardly surprised. It seemed to D'Ayala that he had been waiting ever since childhood for his life to begin. It was always just around the corner, and at any moment some dramatic incident would set the whole thing in motion. What sort of incident? He had no idea. But when it took place, there he would be, awake, aware, surrounded by new ideas and associates, faced with a challenge and shoved by ambition. Alive at last.

As it was, D'Ayala, who was an archivist by profession, felt ashamed that no biographer would care to take on his past. How would the chap select his most fruitful period? His pattern of development? His periods of retrenchment and decline? There hadn't been any. Looking back, D'Ayala knew that he deserved no praise, but felt no blame, either.

Now. Now, right now, was the moment to invite some new experience, to prime the pump. He would approach this American girl displaying her freedom and self-confidence in public in a way that D'Ayala had never before witnessed. Defying a lifetime's custom he left his coffee and went out to her table.

'Can I help you?' he asked.

'Hey, Dad, you speak English!'

'Yes, my mother came from England.'

'No kidding. Mine came from Warsaw. But listen, how could you help me?' she asked, mixing greed and insolence.

'There's a cobbler round the corner, a good one. Would you allow me to show you the way?'

'Hah! No thanks, Dad. I can find my own way round a corner. I'm a big girl now.'

D'Ayala didn't know how to answer, so he inclined his head in the merest suggestion of a bow, and walked back into the bar, standing there selfconscious but pleased. She seemed to have thought that he was making advances to her, and for years nobody had paid him such a compliment.

She had called him 'Dad'. Did he really look so old? Of course he did. At sixty-eight he could have been her grandfather, and his style, with hair brushed smoothly back and clothes meticulously groomed, was that of another age. Yet he didn't feel old. Not at all. Not more than a healthy fifty. What had changed in him since then? Nothing he could pinpoint. His age was just a figure on paper dreamed up by some faraway bureaucrat.

The American girl was getting ready to go. She hauled the rucksack on to a chair, turned her back to it and threaded her arms through the shoulder straps. 'Palermo? I can take it or leave it,' she announced to the world at large, 'and right now I plan to leave it.' She leaned forward, gave a heave and a jerk, stood up with the rucksack comfortably in place, and stumped off into the sunshine.

'I must go home,' thought D'Ayala, swilling the last mouthful of coffee round in his cup and wishing he had been born in a later generation.

D'Ayala went home by way of Piazza Castelnuovo. He stopped on the edge under dusty palms and surveyed it. Who would believe that at night this was a place of cool darkness, empty but for theatregoers? At this time of day it was a sea of cars and coaches, wave upon wave of hot paintwork and chrome through which tourists moved with their arms up like swimmers making for shore. A coach pulled up, looking like a space capsule with tinted windows. Elderly American women stepped bravely from it into the full blast of the mezzogiorno sun, and D'Ayala watched them with admiration. While, at the same time, envying them. He envied all the tourists their energy and their easy self-indulgence manifest in those shiny cars, cameras and comfortable clothes. Most of all he envied their innocent lack of style. He was sure that not one person in that vast square was cramped, as he had been all his life, by iron measures of taste, social elegance, class.

As he left the Piazza, D'Ayala heard behind him the little cries of the American women as they milled about, calling to each other, looking for a sign. 'Where's the flower? Have you seen the flower, honey? We must find it, we have to find it,' and then the anxious note was gone as their calls changed to, 'There it is! Hey, come on, girls, it's right over there,' and they rallied round a dyspeptic academic who held aloft a lily made of plastic.

Chapter 2

D'Ayala's apartment was the entire second floor of a house in Via Mabuse. The house was old and built round a courtyard that gave light to the side rooms. The front of the house was a sullen grey façade with enormous black doors, forbidding as a fortress to the casual passerby but much loved by those privileged to live behind it in the vast rooms that led one into another through high double doors. The D'Ayala family had lived here for generations, adding to the decor as times and tastes changed. The walls were hung with paintings, good and bad, with no more than a thumb's width between them, and dusty putti draped swags of plaster fruit over the doorways. Ornate Sicilian chests in vivid colours fed armies of woodworm. Here and there were small pieces of English furniture of the eighteenth century, contributions from D'Ayala's English mother who, when she saw them set in place after their long journey from Suffolk, could only say, 'Poor things! Poor little things!' In those surroundings they looked like toy furniture, for they lacked the vital drama of the locality.

D'Ayala, turning the corner into Via Mabuse, wished, as he had often done, that he could converse with his mother. If only she would appear, here and now, in the empty street where the two o'clock sun was hammering on the pavement while Palermitans sat shaded at table. He had never been able to believe that she had gone far away, beyond communication of any sort, oblivious of her life on earth. Not that she was looking over his shoulder, exactly, but he felt sure she was nearby, and some kind of *frisson* must reach her when events took place that would have moved her deeply had she been alive. He occasionally recounted events to her as some people do to the bees: who knows what she heard or felt? They had been close, his mother and he, noisily, chattily close, while his father, a man reserved by nature, looked on with amusement from his customary distance and was a little envious of the free expression of this lanky English girl he had brought to Palermo. He had met her at a hunt ball in Suffolk. She had just come down from Oxford and was a little daft with left-wing idealism, and he courted her with outrageously conservative ideas as a kind of shock tactics.

'If you marry me, you'll have farms and labourers right under your heel,' he said, teasing.

'Feudal! I thought as much. I shall come to Sicily and work for the betterment of everyone who pays you rent.'

'They'll be embarrassed.'

'Really?'

'Of course. But won't you come anyway, just for me?' So she had. Letters from her reached northern breakfast tables telling of the mystery and marvels of Sicily, and of the anguish of its poverty, and of her hopeless attempts to organise some local relief. She was, of course, regarded by Palermitans as a typical English eccentric.

Two years after she came to Palermo, Lorenzo was born. Both his parents doted on him and took him to the country often to show him off to his doctor grandfather and to agents and tenants, but his mother secretly looked forward to the time when she and her husband could hold satisfying conversations and exchanges of ideas with their son. She loved him as a baby but she adored him as a youth.

When eventually he went to University in Padua, she was happier than she had ever been. Perhaps she felt that it was a part of her dream for him fulfilled; perhaps she felt that in some way it compensated for the shortfall in her own achievements when first she came to Palermo. Perhaps it was a much shallower satisfaction: like her husband, Lorenzo was good-looking and gorgeously vain, and now that he had left school and was moving in sophisticated circles, she could indulge him with the beginnings of a fine wardrobe. Or could her pleasure have been mainly self-centred, the joy of reliving her time at Oxford? Perhaps it was all of these. Certainly Lorenzo's fellow students liked her. Every vacation found some of them visiting the D'Ayala home. They would arrive with hopeful, sweaty faces and bulging rucksacks, and sleep on parquet floors where tall looking-glasses between the windows mirrored their scattered wash things, clothes, books, maps, sleeping bags and countless sheets of paper bearing notes they had scribbled on Piazza Armerina, Segesta, Sicilian crops, mythology, food and donkeys. Wisely, they had been advised to steer clear of local politics and did so. They all loved to talk, often long into the night. But early next day Lorenzo's parents would come and wake them, dressed in tennis clothes. She would slap her racquet against her thigh like a jockey and say 'Anyone for tennis?' The students could never understand why that question made her laugh. She spoke slowly in a clear voice of the sort that once carried to the ends of the British Empire, and had to be obeyed.

It was during that period that Mariella came to the attention of the D'Ayala family.

Mariella's father was a D'Ayala farm agent. It was his duty to come with the books and figures each week and discuss them with D'Ayala's father, and he began to bring young Mariella with him every time. He and his wife hoped that she would learn some style from what she saw of the D'Ayala household and, as she was now adolescent, they also allowed themselves the hope, the very faintest hope, that she might make an impression on Lorenzo or one of his friends. D'Ayala's father and the agent discussed business for an hour or more at the desk in the study, and Mariella could hardly be left with them, bored to tears. So she was always invited into the drawing-room where D'Ayala's mother felt bound to entertain her. It wasn't easy. They had so little in common, the tall, plain, autocratic Englishwoman with an Oxford degree and socialist tendencies and this pretty, parochial girl who had never wished or needed to think for herself. They sat sipping tea. D'Ayala's mother, hearing herself chat in precisely the way she would have talked to a maid in Suffolk, was embarrassed when she realised it, but was afraid to stop. When she did, they sat like models in a costume museum, smiling, smiling, and communicating nothing.

Lorenzo adored these occasions, although he never let it be known. He wouldn't join their awkward tea party, being at a gawky, selfconscious age himself, but he couldn't resist coming into the room, shaking hands with Mariella and having a quick stare at her.

'Darling, do have some tea with us,' his mother would say, while Mariella smiled at the floor and said not a word.

'Mama, you know I've got work to do. Homework, loads of it,' he would say, already striding towards the door. Once outside he would lean against the wall, close his eyes and submit to the effect of the dewy sexuality that he had just seen creeping out all round the edges of Mariella's dress, the plump silkiness of her elbows and knees, the tops of her breasts, the moist skin of her throat. Only her hands and feet seemed to be under her control: the rest of her seemed to gloat and invite by turns. When Lorenzo closed his eyes and tried to picture Mariella, he didn't see her. He felt her.

One evening at dinner, after such an encounter, his mother said, 'There's a luscious morsel for you, Lorenzo.' Lorenzo blushed and looked down at his plate.

'A luscious morsel?' asked his father idly.

'Mariella, the agent's daughter. Hadn't you noticed?'

'I suppose I hadn't. She must be nearly a grown woman by now.'

'I think she has designs on Lorenzo. She always comes with her father these days, and she's bound to wait for him. She sees him, too – he usually comes to greet her.'

'Mama, I just happened to come in . . .' said Lorenzo.

'Darling, of course you did. You always do. Just don't take her seriously, that's all I ask.'

His father said, 'Come, come, don't be so hard on them. They're only young and like to look at each other. You, of all people, should value the girl for herself alone.'

Lorenzo, too, wondered what had happened to his mother's social conscience. Just for a moment her social awareness seemed to have eclipsed it. She tried to picture the fetching, semi-educated agent's daughter as mistress of the D'Ayala household, representative of the family in the country estates, member of Palermitan society. The picture would not come into focus.

Yet, as it happened, Mariella acquired all those positions before much time had passed.

For Lorenzo's parents were drowned, fishing from a boat off the coast of Ustica one summer's afternoon. Precisely what had happened, nobody knew: D'Ayala himself imagined that his mother must have fallen overboard and his father leapt into the water to help her. She could hardly swim at all, and his father would not have been able to push her big-boned body up over the side of the boat. They must have thrashed about in panic until they died at the foot of those miniature cliffs, only feet high, with stubby little trees on top, and floated lifeless in water so limpid that one could watch jewel-like fish blowing at ripples of sand on the seabed far below. Smoke was still drifting from the boat's smoke stack when a fisherman came upon them, on their backs, hand in hand. From a distance he had thought they were lovers sunbathing.

When this tragedy occurred, Lorenzo was twenty-two and finishing his time at University, and Mariella was nineteen. Within months Mariella's parents began preparations for their wedding, with Lorenzo urging them on.

Now, standing at the corner of Via Mabuse in the heat and desolation of early afternoon in summer, elderly and alone, he wished he had had a chance to explain to his mother. He would like to have said, 'I know you must have hated my marriage to Mariella. To you she was little better than a servant. But that's one reason why I married her. She had known us all for years. You and Father were dead, I was alone, and Mariella was there. What else was there to do? What better consolation than marriage? I was young and full of fantasy: reading for my arts degree had fed it. I had seen human sweetness celebrated by painters and sculptors everywhere, and I knew what instinct and imagination could achieve together. So I planned and yearned and lusted. Mariella and I were to have an epic love-life that would bring us joy every moment of our lives. And what happened? On our wedding night Mariella said, "Oh, Lorenzo, do it the proper way. That's all I like," and flopped over on to her back. She never changed her mind. Or her position, come to that.'

Lorenzo D'Ayala was sure that his mother must have been aware of this, the tragi-comic pinnacle of his young life.

Chapter 3

'The Signora's in the drawing-room,' said Nantica, the housemaid, as she passed D'Ayala in the hall. She was on her way to the dining-table with cutlery and napkins.

'Am I that late?' asked D'Ayala.

'Not really,' said Nantica. 'Signora Bragazzi is often early.'

D'Ayala looked for letters on a console, but there were none. He looked at himself in the looking-glass above it and ran his hand over his hair to smooth it, a useless gesture. He decided that today he looked old. But with no excuse for loitering, he had to go into the drawing-room and greet his guest.

Leila Bragazzi was sitting near the window, neat and upright as befits the daughter of a General. She was in her sixties, and for many years had been Mariella's closest friend and confidante.

'I'm sorry I'm late,' said D'Ayala, and he offered an excuse both impeccable and false. 'I had to finish a little paper I'm working on at the Institute.' D'Ayala had been archivist of the Institute of Fine Arts all his working life. He watched for Leila's tight smile of approval, knowing she valued him most for his profession and its associations. Humdrum was what she thought of him socially.

'Of course,' she said, and immediately felt that she had been too amenable. 'I had a look round while I was waiting,' she said, 'and I don't think Nantica is keeping things up to scratch.'

'Oh, it's all right,' said D'Ayala.

'If you let them get slack, the whole house goes downhill. Then they leave because it's too much work to get it back in order again. And maids are very difficult to get these days, Lorenzo, believe me. A few firm remarks now might save you a lot of trouble in the future.'

'*A tavola!*' screamed Nantica from the dining-room, where all was ready.

'She wouldn't have dared to shout like that if Mariella had been here!' said Leila as she rose from her chair and started towards the dining-room.

The room was large, furnished with glass-fronted cabinets in which silver, glass and porcelain were displayed, and many paintings. A vast table ran down the centre, with high-backed chairs stationed round it. On the day in question the table looked bare; Mariella and Lorenzo D'Ayala had always sat at each end, with Leila Bragazzi at one side, between them. Today Nantica had seated Leila in Mariella's former place, so that guest and host faced each other over a long distance. They shook out their napkins. Nantica put plates in front of them and brought a vast dish laden with pasta.

'Enough for a regiment,' said Leila sarcastically.

'Yes, Signora,' answered Nantica blandly. She had no intention of accepting criticism from a guest, even a guest of such long standing.

When he was a little less hungry, D'Ayala paused and looked down the table at Leila. He wondered why she still came to lunch every Wednesday, just as she had for so many years. It must have been painful with Mariella gone. They had been like sisters: there wasn't a snapshot in the house that didn't show them together. What did Leila need, he wondered, to mark the close of that long relationship? He wanted to help her free herself from the situation, but was afraid of seeming crass.

Leila, for her part, looked down the table and saw the face of D'Ayala as she had not seen him, because she had not truly looked at him, for a long time. It was such an English face, so unnerving. She was used to dark Sicilian faces promising revelations. That English face was open, naked, almost flayed, apparently concealing nothing, which must mean that it concealed everything far more cleverly than one supposed. Yet she had known Lorenzo D'Ayala since he was little more than a boy and he had never taken her by surprise, never seemed more than a mild, bookish man. Her father, the General, had considered him foppish, even namby-pamby. Why, he had even escaped military service in the War. Flat feet, they said. It was a pity that Mariella had not left somebody more entertaining.

The pasta plates disappeared, fresh ones replaced them, and Leila and D'Ayala were served with thin slices of veal.

'I got a letter from my cousins in Adelaide yesterday,' said Leila.

'Ah?'

'They were most upset. They remembered Mariella so well, you know.' She paused to cut her meat. 'Arturo is quite a big-wig these days,' she went on.

'Yes, I suppose so.' D'Ayala's only memory of Arturo was of a pudgy man in an ill-cut Australian suit posing for a photograph in the courtyard of Palazzo Bonagia. Before the war, Arturo had been a good fascist. Even the General regarded him with modest approval.

'... and it looks as if Fabrizio Castiglione will be the mayor of some town in the outback, and Patti and Mina have opened a boutique, fantasy things, you know, all sent over from here because they've no taste out there, really, not really refined taste, Mina says....'

D'Ayala gave up trying to follow. The names became phrases of music formed by Leila's thin lips; whenever she pursed them, tiny wrinkles in the skin radiated outwards, and on the ridges between them the little hairs looked dark. D'Ayala wondered why she so often wore clothes that matched her sandy-coloured hair, making her seem woven from it, head to toe. She was so decent, so dull, and he wished he could like her better.

Come, D'Ayala, how many people do you know in this world whose company is usually a joy? Or even sometimes a joy?

And are you a joy to someone? Dare you give an honest answer?

D'Ayala recalled plenty of occasions on which he had felt cheated. There he would be, looking forward to some meeting with friends, geared up with anticipation, enjoying the first, welcoming handshake. And there he would be at the end of the evening, the time having passed without a hint of interest, wit or, still more to be treasured, affection. The parting handshake would take place in a fog of boredom and disappointment. From recalling such encounters his thoughts moved to relationships, so many over such a long period, that had been stultified from birth, never developing, always hedged about with insincere promises of which he, as much as anyone, was guilty. Those evenings at the opera with Mariella, always on somebody's birthday, always starting with the mention of a single topic that he knew would be safely familiar to everyone, always followed by a sudden reverent hush as the curtain rose and the noisy nonsense began. D'Ayala hated opera.

'So that's about all . . .' Leila was saying. D'Ayala rang for Nantica and told her to bring coffee to the drawing-room. Together, D'Ayala and Leila rose from the table, put down their napkins and moved slowly away through the double doors. In the drawing-room, Nantica had opened one window; it formed a slab of piercing light. The rest of the room was dim and silent, and invited one to rest. Sunk into deep armchairs, holding their coffee cups at chin level, D'Ayala and Leila Bragazzi enjoyed the passing of time.

At last D'Ayala spoke. 'Leila, you mustn't worry about me. Paolo, my own son, doesn't.'

'Then he should. Or has filial duty become another anachronism?'

'He's busy with his own life. He has his son, he has Laura, he has his work in Milan. It's enough.'

One of Leila's earliest memories of Paolo came to her as clearly as if it had been yesterday. Mariella had invited her to walk with her and the little boy in the cool of the public gardens in late afternoon. After a while the two young women sat down on a bench under a pine tree and Paolo began to pick up pine cones from the dust and put them in his pockets. He was squatting so that his knees stuck up between the short trousers of his sailor suit and the tops of his long white socks.

'Paolo,' said Mariella, 'don't play down there. It's dirty. Go and run round that pretty flower bed.' Paolo took no notice. Mariella, her voice edged with vexation, began again. 'Paolo, did you hear me? Get up now, there's a good boy, and go and play near the flower bed.'

'No. I don't want to, I don't want to, I don't want . . .' Leila remembered staring at him, and staring at his knee just by her hand, inviting a slap or a pinch underneath. She remembered the way in which her wrist seemed to lift itself, to prepare itself for the administration of a blow. But then, from the corner of her eye she saw Mariella looking at her in amazement tinged with hate. At once she dropped her wrist to her lap again, trying not to blush, staring into the distance. But she never forgot that moment, the shock of the hatred, the guilt of a small act of barbarism never committed.

'In any case,' Lorenzo was saying, 'I don't need to bother Paolo. As you see, I'm well. I have an excellent doctor if I need one. And the Institute is a kind of second home – I've been there over forty years now. It provides me with friends, a little work, interesting correspondence. What more can I need?'

Leila wanted to find a pleasant memory of Paolo, a soothing, charming moment from his past. She would not have liked Lorenzo – and still less, Mariella – to have known that her memories of their only son's past were all inclined to be disagreeable, although, truth to tell, she suspected that neither of them had had much joy from him at any age. Even at eleven or twelve years old he had been remarkably friendless, running straight home from school on his own and then, finding himself lonely, clinging tiresomely to his mother and any afternoon visitors she might have. Securing Mariella's attention for any length of time had been quite a luxury in those days if Paolo was around.

Leila's clearest memory of Paolo in adolescence was of his legs dangling over the arm of a sofa while he lay back, staring at the ceiling and smoking. There was none of the electric energy and marvellous foolhardiness of youth about him, and he did not amuse or endear himself to anyone. Mariella did not talk about him, but about his problems. It was just as well that drugs had not been commonplace at that period.

Eventually he took a law degree. He was fond of looking back on that period as an error in his parents' judgement and a waste of time and energy, producing nothing but a piece of paper with no relevance to life. But without it where would he have been? Not even his father's name and influence could get him a better position than secretary to the wine syndicate, where he had been ever since and about which he never ceased to grumble.

The most astonishing fact of Paolo's life was his marriage to Laura. Why had she ever accepted him? The mystery, as with all marriages, was never solved, but he did represent financial security and stable family ties. Fussy, elegant and always irritated, Laura ran their home and brought up their child and, when she was feeling goodnatured and ambitious, tried to help Paolo to view the world broadly and not as an arena crowded with picadors. For her pleasure she took lovers, to keep herself busy she organised the Condominium tennis club. Leila wondered if Laura could keep up her frantic life indefinitely. It was just as well that one couldn't foresee the future. Leila thought it wise to change the subject.

'What about the maids?' she asked.

'They look after me very well.'

'I hope they stay,' she said. 'They don't usually like a household without a mistress. It obliges them to think for themselves.'

'If they leave me, I shall ask for your help,' said D'Ayala, smiling gently. He had, without difficulty, released Leila from her duty lunches, and she knew it. The two of them sat back, pleased with each other, closer than they had been for years. For a time they were drowsy and silent.

Then Leila said, 'Lorenzo, it's time I went home. I'm playing bridge at five o'clock. Will you call me a cab?'

When the cab came, D'Ayala accompanied Leila to the door, kissed her cheek and watched her go downstairs holding the bannister. She had lost the courage to be agile. When she had moved carefully round the corner, out of sight, he waited for a moment before closing the door.

He then went to his study. He sat down at his desk, and took from the top drawer a large, battered address book bound in shabby leather. He opened it. His mother's handwriting was there, his father's, too. Mariella's small script. His own. And a few entries made by Paolo as a boy.

D'Ayala read, from start to finish, every name in the book. He turned back to the beginning. He took up his pen. He began to strike out name after name. Everyone who bored him. Everyone who left him feeling depressed. Everyone who was no more than a duty. Everyone with whom his relationship was static or barren. He was amazed to see how many people his pen, which seemed to have become mechanical judge as well as executioner, smoothly exterminated.

The deed done, he slammed the book shut.

Chapter 4

Nantica was arranging D'Ayala's breakfast tray. She put on it a roll and butter, sugar, a small cup and saucer. On the stove a Neapolitan coffee pot was hissing towards its safety limit: she had blocked the steam vent with a matchstick to make the pressure build up, swell the coffee grains and strengthen the resultant elixir. She turned to the pot, listened to it, and suddenly took its twin handles between her index fingers and thumbs and turned the whole contraption upside down. Boiling water that had been in the lower half was now aloft and began to filter down through the grains, extracting their aromatic oils, colour and power to set the nervous system on course for the day. When every drop was in the lower half of the pot, Nantica replaced the upper half with a lid. The coffee was ready. She put it on the tray and went to D'Ayala's door on which she knocked with one hand, balancing the tray on the other. Without waiting for a reply, she went in, crossed the gloomy room to a table by the window, and set down the tray. She drew back the curtains and opened the window towards her.

Now came the high spot of her ritual. With a clatter of iron latches she released the louvred shutters and, like a swimmer breasting water, leaned out of the window spreading her arms and pushing the shutters aside until they hit the outside walls.

In so doing, Nantica presented her bottom full-on, at eye-level, to D'Ayala, who lay in bed awaiting this moment every morning.

'Thank you, Nantica,' he said. 'What sort of a day is it?'

'Beautiful,' she said, straightening up, and she went out of the room, leaving him to his morning routine.

Wrapped in a favourite old dressing-gown, D'Ayala sat at the table and ate his breakfast. The coffee was magical: within minutes he felt like a new man. He padded across the floor to his bathroom and drew his bath: torrents of water from giant brass taps crashed down into the steamy depths of a relic of nineteenth century comfort.

D'Ayala lounged in the water. He hummed some Beethoven.

Swaddled in a towel, he shaved, scrutinised his face from several angles in a hinged mirror, and combed his hair.

He then selected clothes for the day. Fresh underwear. A silk shirt bearing, on the left breast, his monogram embroidered in tiny crimson stitches, the whole design little bigger than a fingernail. He chose a silk tie to match the monogram. He smoothed pale grey silk socks over his bony ankles. On the previous evening, Nantica had wheeled a wooden 'dead man' into the room wearing a suit newly sponged and pressed: D'Ayala donned the suit. It hung well, cut by his Palermitan tailor from first-rate English cloth. D'Ayala pocketed the top layer from a pile of linen handkerchiefs with hand-rolled hems. He took a pair of shoes from their trees, slid his feet into them, noted how well they fitted his narrow English feet, made as they were on his own last in soft Italian leather.

D'Ayala was dressed.

In a pierglass he examined the total ensemble. It was gorgeous, and yet discreet, without any hint of *bella figura* about it. It was also absurdly old-fashioned, labour-intensive and unpractical. D'Ayala's modern tourist would have found it a lot of nonsense. Laughable nonsense, in all probability.

Nantica came to the door. 'Dottore, there are two Sisters to see you. They're waiting in the hall.'

'Nantica, have you told them that I'm leaving for my office this very minute?'

'I told them. But they wouldn't go away.' Nantica, annoyed

that she had lost in a skirmish with the nuns, hoped that D'Ayala would avenge her.

The Sisters greeted D'Ayala in whispers as if they felt that grief had made him too fragile to bear ordinary talk. 'Ah, Dottore, Dottore. . . .' Then, couched in soft, plaintive sounds came a demand for money, funds to retrieve Mariella's soul from Purgatory and send it on its way to Paradise. The idea that Mariella, so dull and ordinary, could be guilty and in need of purification, struck D'Ayala as absurd.

'Dear Sisters, you're surely not talking about my wife?' he asked. He couldn't think of a more blameless being. As for the suggestion that earthly wealth could affect her supranatural destiny, he found that ludicrous.

But the nuns persisted. Behind the whispers, the prayer-like entreaties, were wills of steel. And D'Ayala, finding it too early in the day for serious argument, wrote a modest cheque and gave it to them in a spirit of genuine hypocrisy. Satisfied, one of them slid the cheque into the folds of her habit while the other hissed a blessing at him. He watched them descend the stairs, black brides steeped in a gloomy faith that seemed ill-suited to lands made brilliant by the Mediterranean sun.

D'Ayala went to his study. The address book was still lying on top of the desk. He opened it and was surprised at what he had done. 'Am I so violent a man?' he asked himself. Turning the pages, he became depressed. All the names there – those he had spared and those he had not – drew him back into the past. There was nothing for the new D'Ayala, the would-be modern, until he noticed the name 'George Kaplan'. Then his mood changed in an instant.

Kaplan flashed into his mind's eye, standing by the road from Poggibonsi on a summer's day in 1929. Kaplan flagged him down. Kaplan, aged twenty-three, addressed D'Ayala, who was twenty, as 'sir' because D'Ayala was driving his own Fiat.

'Hello, good morning, sir, can you give me a lift?' Kaplan, small and dark and unquestionably Jewish, stood beside a rucksack that was almost as tall as he was. He wore lederhosen, thick green socks, and heavy boots. His glance was piercing, his smile irresistible.

'Yes, of course. Can you ride in the dicky? My books are all over the front seat. I'm going to San Gimignano, by the way.'

'Perfect,' said Kaplan, and he heaved his rucksack into the dicky and jumped into the small space that was left.

D'Ayala drove off, crashed the gears, laughed, sped like a fiend down the road. Ecstasy was being a university student on holiday in his own, albeit second-hand, car – his first – with a cheerful companion. Kaplan, wind-blown in the dicky, was bellowing Schubert at the top of his voice. Eventually he stopped and shouted, 'I see the towers, the towers of San Gimignano.'

'We'll be there in a minute,' shouted D'Ayala. The little Fiat chuntered through the city gates and pulled up in a square. D'Ayala got out. Kaplan, as in a trance, sat with his head back over the edge of the dicky, staring up at towers and sky and darting swallows.

'Are you coming with me?' asked D'Ayala.

'Where to?' asked Kaplan.

'To look at the Gozzoli frescoes. I'm an art student.'

'Then I'll come too.'

They left the rucksack in the car and started down a narrow street that ran the length of the village. Long-legged D'Ayala strode. Kaplan seemed to bounce along beside him. As they went, he supplied snippets of information about himself: his father was a Viennese doctor, he himself was a student at Heidelberg, reading philosophy. His politics were left wing.

At the end of the village, the street opened on to a bare, sunny square at the far side of which stood the church of St Augustine on a plinth of shallow steps. A man with a besom was sweeping them. He stopped to have a good look at the two young men as they passed him and went into the church, and he decided that they were well-to-do and could be useful to him. But he must have patience.

Inside the church it was dark, but D'Ayala led the way down the nave and round behind the altar into the apse. An old priest shuffled in to join them from the vestry, carrying two large candles. D'Ayala gave him some money, and then held up the candles to light the walls. The frescoes appeared, glowing, luminous, in brilliant colours and life.

Kaplan said nothing for a minute. Then he commented, 'So Christians whip even their saintly babies.'

One of the frescos showed St Augustine as a small boy at school about to be beaten. He was held piggyback by a big youth, his buttocks were bare, and he was looking back over his shoulder at a calm man with a bunch of twigs who was about to inflict the punishment.

'Surely everyone punishes naughty children?' said D'Ayala.

'Punishments vary,' said Kaplan. 'Christians are devoted to pain and death.'

'Oh, come now....'

Not many years had to pass before D'Ayala was forced to concede Kaplan's point. But in that place at that time everything seemed for the best in the best of all possible worlds. The two young men came out of the church into dazzling sunshine and paused on the top step. The sweeper was still at work, but when he saw them he stopped and came over to them, carrying his besom on his shoulder like a rifle.

'Signori, good morning,' he said. 'Excuse me for accosting you like this, but I have something I think you should see. Come with me. You won't regret it.'

'What is it?' asked D'Ayala.

'Signori, it is a painting, a fine painting, the kind one dreams of hanging in one's house.'

'Where did you get it from?' asked Kaplan, already curious.

'My family, Signori, my family have always had it. They say it was a gift from the painter himself, long ago. But now I must sell it.' The sweeper's voice dropped. 'I have seven children and another on the way, so many mouths to feed, Signori, innocent mouths....'

D'Ayala had heard such tales many times in Sicily and often had a look at the 'painting' in question. It had always turned out to be a crude copy made by the vendor himself, or a print, or even a colour-page torn from a magazine and framed.

'We haven't time today,' said D'Ayala, and he started to walk away.

'No, wait a moment, I'd like to look at it,' said Kaplan. 'Don't go just yet. Sit here and wait for me. I shan't be long.'

'You'll be robbed,' warned D'Ayala.

But Kaplan was determined. The sweeper's forlorn face perked up as soon as he realised this, and he led the foreign visitor across the square to his house.

D'Ayala sat on the steps in the sun waiting, but not for long. Kaplan came back alone across the square, humming and carrying a parcel wrapped in newspaper under his arm. He sat down beside D'Ayala, undid the paper and said, 'Look at this. It's really very fine.'

D'Ayala, dubious, was already framing a gentle criticism in his mind that would not be tactless or upsetting but would indicate to Kaplan that his acquisition was of little value. When he saw it, however, he was surprised. The painting was no old master, but a competent nineteenth century craftsman's work, oils on board, and the subject was a favourite: a little Madonna, romantic and decorative.

'She's very pretty,' said D'Ayala. 'You've got a nice find there. But how much did you pay?'

'All the money I had left,' said Kaplan cheerfully. 'Now I haven't a penny-piece.' So D'Ayala had to lend him money, and that loan sealed their friendship. It was repaid a year later in Vienna by Kaplan's father who smiled up through his pince-nez at this tall young visitor from Italy.

That was the first of several visits to Vienna that D'Ayala remembered with pleasant awe. Kaplan's father was well known among Viennese intellectuals in the nineteen twenties, not only as a doctor with special interest in psychology, but also as a gifted amateur musician and classicist. Until the fascists made foreign travel difficult, especially for Jews, Kaplan's father and his friends played games of wits such as sending cables to each other when abroad posing riddles in Latin and Greek. In such company D'Ayala developed new tastes and sophistication, especially in music. Hardly an evening passed by without chamber music in Kaplan's father's house or a concert in the city.

Kaplan himself visited Palermo several times during University vacations, staying in the D'Ayala household and entertaining everyone with accounts of Vienna, the exploits and idiosyncracies of his father's friends, and news of the musical world. He also travelled over Sicily's dusty roads and flower-strewn fields to visit Segesta and Selinunte, Piazza Armeria, Agrigento, Siracusa. Sometimes he went alone, more often he went with D'Ayala in the little car, and he was always, no matter how hard the journeys nor how primitive the bed and board, overjoyed with Sicily and his Sicilian companion. 'Lorenzo, you live in paradise!' he would crow, 'and you share it with me!'

They came from such different worlds, these two young men, but they complemented each other. D'Ayala found that Kaplan, although a good student of history, was essentially a man of the future who delighted in progress and modernity; Kaplan admired D'Ayala's knowledge of art, his feeling for the past, and the sense of stability these gave him. Each fulfilled intellectual needs in the other. Thus their friendship grew and flourished, surviving even D'Ayala's marriage to Mariella.

'Kaplan,' D'Ayala told her when they had been married for a few months, 'is an Austrian Jew and I love him.'

'Well, don't bring him here,' she answered with a sniff.

'Why ever not?'

'Because I don't want to know him. He's a foreigner twice over.'

D'Ayala forbore to remind her that Sicily is a colourful mixture of races and creeds. From then on D'Ayala and Kaplan preserved their relationship with letters.

Letters from Kaplan, however, grew fewer and more guarded as time went by, and in late 1939 they ceased altogether. D'Ayala tried not to dwell on the probable reason, to hope for an optimistic explanation and, in dark moods, to put Kaplan out of his mind altogether. He himself, told that because his feet were flat he could not serve in the Forces, suffered extra humiliation when he found himself fussing over dusty papers at the Institute while troops younger than he were fighting for their lives on the Sicilian coast and arriving in Palermitan hospitals maimed and disfigured. Even Mariella was allowed to demonstrate more physical courage than he: she gave birth to Paolo, their only child, with only their maids in attendance.

Then, towards the end of 1943, a letter arrived, stamped, franked, marked with crayon by the censor and ink by the

Red Cross, dog-eared, thumb-marked, but with D'Ayala's name and address just legible and a sheet of paper inside giving Kaplan's news. He was in England, had been there since August, 1939, and was a serving soldier in the Pioneer Corps.

'Building bridges, my dear,' the letter ran. 'Can you imagine it? The only bridges I ever tackled in my whole life were the sort you find in translations from German to English. I shan't win any medals.'

The war ended and Kaplan was demobbed. He joined a publishing house, and later acquired one of his own. On rare visits to London, doing a little research for the Institute at the British Museum or visiting English relations, D'Ayala always stayed with Kaplan and Miriam, his wife, and Bernard, their son, at their house in Wimbledon, enjoying a brief whirl of socialising, concerts, theatres and talk.

But one day, not long before Mariella's death, a letter had arrived from Kaplan in an envelope edged with black. It read:

> Lorenzo, my dear, I have lost my wife. Miriam died from a stroke two days ago. She was so good, such a *mensch*, and such a good mother to Bernard that nothing can ever be the same again.
>
> The funeral is tomorrow at the Jewish cemetery in Golders Green. Of course you cannot be there, but I shall think of you and the happiness you brought her with your visits.
>
> Although we meet so seldom, I always think of you with a regard as warm as that of your Sicilian sun.
>
> Kaplan

And now? Mariella, too, was gone. D'Ayala was free to visit or entertain anyone he wished. He wondered if it was too late.

That evening, as soon as he had dined, he went to his study and wrote a long letter to Kaplan in London.

Chapter 5

The Institute of Fine Arts had drifted through years of pleasant obscurity providing positions, some of them little more than sinecures, for generations of good Sicilian families. Through its portals one caught a glimpse of an uninviting courtyard with dusty windows. From time to time a lecture was given in one of its handsome rooms under crumbling baroque plaster; thus D'Ayala or a colleague could air a hobby-horse for an hour while justifying the existence of the Institute before an audience who were all deeply bored.

Like so much in Sicily, the Institute was unchanging, unable to change, hostile to the very idea of change. So, under the new Director, it was bound to suffer.

The new Director was young, clever, not at all refined, a political appointee from Rome installed over the heads of existing Institute staff without consultation. He cared nothing about art, was chary of the Mafia, and looked at the economics of the Institute with a banker's cold eye. Modernisation and redundancies threatened.

The new Director stopped for coffee on his way to the Institute one morning. He leaned against the bar, thinking. He needed a woman.

'Another coffee,' he said to the barman.

The Director enjoyed challenge or, to be exact, the total

victory he usually won from it. With subordinates he was merciless: he liked to override them and then watch them shrink. He thought about his secretary, Annamaria Schindt. He pictured her back view, standing at the files in his office with her pointed shoulderblades nearly as prominent as her nipples, and her pinchpenny buttocks clamped together by a narrow skirt, and he longed to rape her.

As he reached down the bar counter for some sugar he saw at the window, peering in over the top of boxes of chocolates and pyramids of cakes, the face of D'Ayala. The Director flinched. D'Ayala, alone of all the Institute staff, had so far proved invincible. In the first place, he was protected by that aura of class and the formality of his manners. The Director, feeling his social inferiority keenly, could not bring himself to be as unpleasant as he would have liked. In the second place, D'Ayala did not fit the Director's idea of an Englishman or half-Englishman at all. He was not slow or stupid, he was not the natural prey for Sicilian shopkeepers and pickpockets, he was nobody's fool. Did his Sicilian blood alone give him the authority he brought to his work? It was hard to believe. The Director had, from time to time, set little traps for him, but they never worked. D'Ayala was an excellent archivist.

At the moment in question, moreover, the Director felt a special loathing for D'Ayala because the archivist had caught him off-guard, submerged in sexual fantasy, with his physical excitement probably discernible right through the window. The Director felt sweat trickle down his body and his heart go wild with adrenalin. He forced a smile on to his face and raised his hand in a childish wave.

D'Ayala was disappointed. He had been looking forward to a cup of coffee but could not inflict discomfiture on the Director, so he gave a pleasant nod and went on his way to the Institute. At once the Director fled to the lavatory.

He emerged, stomach in, chest expanded, zip on its way up, a man reassured. During those moments before the tiles, the thought had occurred to him that D'Ayala could now be fired. A decent interval had elapsed since the funeral of D'Ayala's wife, and his new status could at last be acknowledged: he was no longer a husband, but an ageing widower, not head of a family, but an elderly relative, not master of his household, but an old man cared for by servants. Anyone could see that it was time he left the Institute. The Director began to plan a letter to Rome '. . . our revered Professor . . . we ask too much . . . young men must shoulder the burden . . .' It was easy. As soon as he arrived at the Institute, he began to put it down on paper.

Chapter 6

The days of high summer were passing slowly and Palermo baked. Most members of the Institute staff went on holiday and those who remained looked forward to the cool promenades of evening. D'Ayala waited for a letter from Kaplan and wished that life would change a little.

One day it did. D'Ayala came home to find his cook sitting on her suitcase in the hall amid string bags and paper parcels all prepared for a journey.

'Dottore, I can't go on any more, it's too much for me with the Signora gone and having to buy what I think and watching over everything and not having anyone to ask. What's more, my feet are murdering me.' She held up one of the offending feet with its corns and bunions protruding between the straps of worn sandals, its toenails brown and ribbed and curving into the flesh, its plump heel supported precariously by the sandal's narrow back. 'Torment,' she said, putting the foot down again. 'Ask Nantica, she knows what I've suffered. You're a good man, Dottore, but I can't manage all the extra. I just want to go back to Trapani.'

D'Ayala saw that those feet must have been the cause of much bad temper in the kitchen, year in and year out, and that their effect on him had been nothing more than irritation at the sounds of squabbling. Had Mariella noticed them, he wondered? They could have sent the cook to their doctor, but they had done nothing. It was not one of their obligations, attending to the cook's feet, Mariella would have said. His mother would at least have tried some home remedy.

'You should have told me before,' he said gently.

'Yes, but there it is, I didn't have the courage.' On her face was the expression worn by martyrs in cinquecento paintings.

'Where will you stay in Trapani tonight? Does anyone know you're coming?' In the back of his mind D'Ayala had a tenant farmer not far from Trapani who would put her up for a day or two.

'My brother, Dottore. I can go to him. He fishes at night, so I'll use his bed.'

D'Ayala gave her some money and sent Nantica to help her with her luggage to the bus out of Palermo.

Nantica, younger and more resourceful, managed to run the D'Ayala household on her own, maintaining its customary style for about a month. Then she had to admit that it was too much work for her and that, strangely, she missed the cook's temper. It had been an effective goad. She stayed a little longer, with D'Ayala's persuasion, but she cooked less and less, let the house run down, and had to struggle to keep D'Ayala's wardrobe in trim. She murmured more and more often about crops maturing on her father's farm and the shortage of hands to gather them in, and eventually she, too, packed her bags and went home weeping, not only because she was losing a good house to live in and a kind employer, but also because she had not found herself a husband in Palermo and was still only half-way through assembling a dowry.

D'Ayala managed by himself well enough for the first few days without servants, but when he discovered that his stock of clean shirts was running out he felt a little desperate. His mother and Mariella would both have found new maids among the tenant farmers' families, girls who would have rejoiced to leave the land and come to big-city Palermo and work in a grand house, just as Nantica had done. But this was no longer so. Domestic help was hard to find, he was told, just as Leila Bragazzi had warned. In any case he didn't relish the long procedures followed by his mother and wife in taking on a new servant, the journeys to the country, the letters, the recommendation from the local priest, the feudal promises and pledges.

Instead, D'Ayala went to see his tailor.

The tailor fancied himself a man of the world, and was flattered to be consulted by D'Ayala. 'Dottore, I understand perfectly. No gentleman can be expected to take care of his house and his wardrobe. You need a good, hard-working girl to see to everything for you. A willing girl.' He smiled. 'A decorative girl, too, why not? Why should life be dull?' The tailor knew he was taking a risk, but it was irresistible to him to see how far he could push familiarity with a customer of long standing, especially since, at that very moment, he had in his workroom two boys learning his trade and he was sure they laughed at him behind his back and thought him fuddy-duddy. A little refined sexy banter with a gentleman as impressive as D'Ayala would answer them, he thought, better than a straight brag about his manhood.

D'Ayala, however, was uncomfortable and protested, 'No, no, just an ordinary domesticated woman. Who irons well,' he added.

The tailor was abashed. He frowned exaggeratedly. He portrayed deep, grave thought. Then he said, like one who has seen the light, 'Ah, Dottore, there's no problem! No problem at all! You must employ my niece, Alba, a fine girl in need of a position in a good house, and reformed.'

'Reformed?' asked D'Ayala.

'Reformed by the Sisters,' said the tailor proudly. 'To the highest standards. And fully trained in domestic work.'

It seemed that Alba was the eldest child in a large country family so poor that they had to share their shelter with their animals and, as soon as Alba reached fourteen years old, she was dumped in a Palermo street and left to find her own living. This she did with ease, taking to prostitution. After a while the police picked her up and put her in the care of nuns. Now she was fully grown, a good, healthy Christian girl.

'And what a worker!' added the tailor. 'Like a donkey – without need for a stick. You'll never find anyone better, Dottore. What's more, she won't be greedy for wages – she's used to a very simple life with the Sisters. All that needs to be done is for me to visit them, give a little money to the Order, let my niece have some for expenses, travel... and that's it. You'll be well cared for, and so will your house.'

Even as the tailor spoke, D'Ayala was feeling for his wallet and counting out notes. He gave generously, glad that the matter had been settled so quickly.

'Tell Alba – you said that was her name? – to come to my house tomorrow morning early. I shall be expecting her.'

The next morning as he was dressing, D'Ayala saw from his window a girl standing in the street below looking up at the house. She wore a shapeless home-made dress, and between her feet she had stood her suitcase, a shoddy thing made of cardboard, but she wasn't going to let it be stolen. Examining the severe face of D'Ayala's home, she wondered whether to bolt, and D'Ayala could see the doubt in her face and sense the anxious tensing of her body. Before she could take flight, he must reach her. He snatched up his dressing-gown and hurried downstairs.

She was still there in the road, looking up, plucking uncertainly at the sides of her skirt.

'Alba? Are you Alba?'

'Yes, and you are the Dottore?'

'That's right. Come in.'

She paused for a second, wondering again whether to run for it, back into the alleys where she belonged, with boarded, cobwebby windows and the clamour of radios and argument and hungry children.

'Just come in and look, Alba. And make us a good cup of coffee.' He was smiling, not leering, and he kept his hands to himself. She was eaten up with curiosity; she had never been inside one of these grand houses. Slowly she picked up the suitcase and followed him. As she did so, she studied his back with the eye of a connoisseur, noticing the way his robe clung to him, outlining buttocks that drooped and thighs as narrow as calves. These were the sad signs of old age. She had known old men. They were slow and gentle in bed, and some of them wept if they had no erection. She didn't want another old man. She preferred to do the housework.

When they reached the hall, Alba put down her suitcase and looked at D'Ayala, front view. 'Now this one,' she said to herself, 'is different.'

He still kept his robe closed, so he wasn't a client. On the other hand, he wasn't like any of the priests she had known. Instead of their thin, vinegary, unwashed smell, there floated from D'Ayala an aroma of luxury, and his hands were bony and tanned, not the moist pink extremities of those who finger what they claim is flesh yet have never touched the living organs of women. D'Ayala, decided Alba, belonged to a category that she had not yet encountered. He was a true gentleman.

'Sit here while I go and dress, Alba,' he was saying. 'Then I'll show you the apartment, and you can decide whether or not you'd like to look after it for me.'

Alba hesitated to sit on one of the gilt chairs with their showy legs and embroidered scenes – from the lives of martyrs, Sicilian legends, ancient battles? They were all, in any case, pictures of men in some male activity. So instead she perched on the top of her suitcase, and looked about her from this safe, homely position. What she saw first impressed and cowed her, but in minutes it began to have a warm and cheerful effect on her spirits. So much colour, so much gold, such cool marble table tops to rest one's hands on in summer, she liked it all, and not for the usual reasons. She realised, for instance, that console tables don't get in the way when one is washing the floor beneath them, and that, in fact, there wasn't much floor to be noticed, well or badly washed, with so much furniture about the place.

The hall of the Convent where she had lived with the nuns had been bleak and enormous, revealing the exact extent of one's efforts and energy when it had been scrubbed. The visitors' waiting-room had not been much better. It had hard, straight-backed chairs and one small statue of St Sebastian, prickly with arrows, in the corner. She could still remember the voice of the Sister in charge whispering, 'No child, clean nothing but the floor. I shall see to everything else.' That night Alba had dreamed that Sister snatched off St Sebastian's loin cloth and flicked a duster with painful venom at his marble genitals.

At last D'Ayala, dressed, came into the hall. Alba noted how well her uncle, the tailor, had disguised the drooping buttocks and thin thighs by ingenious cutting of the cloth.

'I'm sorry I kept you waiting, Alba,' said D'Ayala. The apology surprised her. She stood up awkwardly and picked up her suitcase. 'Leave your suitcase here while I show you round,' he said. She pushed it under a table, out of sight. It looked more rubbishy and worn out than ever in these surroundings.

D'Ayala enjoyed showing Alba the apartment. She had never seen anything like it. 'It's a palazzo!' she kept saying as he opened doors and led her into rooms where noble furniture was arrayed on polished parquet floors and nobody had ever known what it was to go hungry.

They came, eventually, to the kitchen; like the Convent kitchen, it had cracked white tiles and yards of gas and water pipes. The nuns had given Alba the task of cleaning tiles and pipes, gouging grease out from behind them with an old, broken knife. But here there were no nuns, Alba would be boss, and the grease could stay where it was, undisturbed.

Beyond the kitchen was a linen-room with floor-to-ceiling cupboards and rails of hangers for shirts. Ironing equipment, buttons, needle and thread were all ready for use. On a 'dead man' hung a suit. Alba was impressed.

The next room was the first of the maids' bedrooms. Alba looked in and her face fell. The room was like a cell, and when D'Ayala peered in over her shoulder he felt quite ashamed.

'Alba, this is ridiculous. Come and choose yourself a decent room, for heaven's sake.'

She did, fetching her suitcase from the hall and dumping it on the bed of a guestroom with its own bathroom, unused for some time. Alba played with the taps and through the perished rubber of the shower hose came needles of rusty-red water. It didn't matter. The idea of having her own bathroom was glamour enough. D'Ayala, watching her, was careful to keep all thoughts of Mariella and his mother out of his head, or so he thought. In fact, he could hear their comments. It was easy to imagine what they would say.

'Really, Lorenzo, do you know what you're doing? Giving

this little slut of a girl one of the best rooms in the house – probably in all Palermo – when you know nothing about her whatsoever! The tailor's niece, you say? She's probably his little whore. Dirty, too. God knows what she'll bring into the house with her. And what will visitors say, when they find they have to sleep in the second guest-room because the maid, yes, the *maid* is queening it in the best room in the house? What does she want with that bathroom, anyway? There's a perfectly good bathroom for the maids at the end of the corridor. And those cupboards with the inlaid doors – your grandmother had them put there, they're priceless – and this girl will throw into them nothing but rubbish and she'll bang the doors shut and never make the bed properly and soon everything in that room will smell. Lorenzo, have you taken leave of your senses? Send her away now, before she makes herself at home.' So, he was sure, would say Mariella.

D'Ayala's mother was little better. Yet again she would ride her socialist charger to the very brink of immediate reality and then, at the last moment, fall back weakly into the attitudes of her upbringing. 'Darling,' she would say, 'if you give the girl that room she'll get ideas above her station. Yes, I know everyone deserves decent living conditions, I've always said so, but there's really nothing wrong with the maids' rooms and nobody ever said we should each have a palace. She might come to regard the apartment as hers as much as yours, and start bringing in her friends. It could be frightfully awkward. Besides, do you really want her using the bath in there? That's so personal, you know. Guests might not like to use it after her. You see, I don't expect her to stay too long, not by herself at her age.'

Firmly, D'Ayala dismissed his wife and mother. 'Come and make us some coffee, Alba,' he said, and they went back to the kitchen together. There D'Ayala watched Alba handle the coffee machine with all the deftness he lacked. 'You do that like an expert,' he said. 'Will you really stay and keep house for me?'

'How much will you pay me, Dottore?' she asked.

D'Ayala had not thought out the matter of wages, and consequently he promised her a sum that was over-generous.

As he heard the words leave his mouth, he realised that Mariella would have been quite scandalised.

'Hm,' said Alba. 'O.K. For that I'll do the lot. You won't need any other women.' D'Ayala smiled, and the appointment was settled.

That evening Alba ironed shirts in the linen-room and considered what she had learned about D'Ayala so far. His prime interest was his wardrobe. It would be easy to keep him contented: she liked washing and, although she had never ironed shirts before, she would soon discover the tricks. She looked down at the shirt lying on the ironing board at that moment, its chest upwards, the collar tilted back over the end, the two sleeves hanging down to the floor, limp and helpless. Ah yes, Alba could take care of this man.

She stopped thinking about D'Ayala and began instead to sing, bringing forth the long, wailing lines of a traditional song from her own district and setting updated words to them. Lovers sailed to America, bought microwave ovens and hi fi, made fortunes out of salty crackers and new airlines. D'Ayala, reading in his study, half-heard the song and thought she was singing of mediaeval heroes and derring-do.

From then on Alba took very good care of D'Ayala's wardrobe and neglected the housework. She polished what took her fancy and let the rest gather dust. Who would notice or care? Whole rooms in the apartment were never used at all.

She was puzzled, however, by D'Ayala's life style. Here was a vigorous, healthy man who spent time reading and writing. Although he was rich, he had no television set and went to work daily like a common labourer. He addressed her more politely than a priest and thanked her for services for which he paid her well. Strangest of all, he ate his meals in a vast room, silent and alone.

'Dottore, do you like eating alone?' asked Alba one evening as she cleared the table.

'I hate it,' he said.

'Then why don't I eat with you?'

D'Ayala was flummoxed. If she had suggested sharing his bed, he would have been less so. But sharing a table, dressed and seated apart, was unthinkable.

He sought a delicate way to refuse her suggestion. Mariella would have said no, point blank. His mother would have felt uncomfortable, but found some excuse to refuse. How silly of them both, he thought. Who wants to be alone? Who wants to forego the cheerful company of the young? He should be flattered that this pretty girl wanted to be with him.

'Tomorrow, Alba, we dine together,' he said.

Chapter 7

Next evening Alba set two places at D'Ayala's dining-table. She had cooked a good dinner, but before serving it she went to her room, took off the dress provided by the nuns, and kicked it under the bed.

Watching herself in the mirror, she began to dress in new clothes bought with her first wages, pushing her arms through the sleeves of a red shirt stiff with that dressing used to give cheap, flimsy material more body and appeal on a market stall. The dressing was scratchy and smelled unpleasant, but Alba wrinkled her nose and put up with it because she knew it would disappear as soon as she washed the shirt. Jeans came next, stiff as boards, and Alba had to yank at them, struggle, wriggle and heave to get them on. She pushed the bottom of the shirt inside the jeans, dragged up the zip, and gave a little sigh of satisfaction. From a paper bag she took gold sandals and slid her feet into them. It was time for a last session at the mirror, trying to see herself from every angle. She liked what she saw, and went to the kitchen to fetch dinner.

D'Ayala actually heard the jeans as Alba came towards the dining-room since they gave a faint percussive accompaniment to every step that she took. When he saw her in her complete outfit, he was astounded. Alba, the nuns' girl, had become a sexy modern woman like a tourist.

'You've got new clothes, Alba. Nice, very nice.'

She smiled and stuck out her breasts against the red shirt. As soon as the dishes were on the table she sat down and began to eat without preliminaries, leaning low over her plate to cram the pasta into her mouth, and as she did so D'Ayala found himself looking into the warm, dark cleft between her breasts. Suddenly he realised that he had not shared a meal with an attractive woman since he was a young man. In that moment, D'Ayala began to covet Alba with a surge of longing.

From that evening on, D'Ayala was relieved to find the table set for two. He had feared that Alba might leave him for a more exciting job or a young admirer, but there she was, joining him with cheerful talk and appalling table manners. He remembered the strictures of his mother on this last point, and smiled.

One evening Alba said, 'Dottore, why don't you have a television set?'

'I've never needed one,' said D'Ayala. 'I read a lot. My wife did needlework.'

'Needlework?' Alba shrank inwardly, remembering the heaps of mending that she had done for the nuns, one of whom had taught her to patch sheets, darn stockings, mend things worn so thin that they were not worth the thread, never mind the labour. Almost every time that that nun looked over her shoulder at the work in her hands, she said, 'Unpick it and do it again. You can surely do it better than that. It's a disgrace.'

Alba looked at D'Ayala anxiously. 'What needlework?' she asked.

'Very fine work,' said D'Ayala, 'pictures in coloured silks and wools. They took many months, sometimes years, to finish.'

'I hate needlework,' said Alba.

'Then don't do any. It just happened to be my wife's passion.'

Mariella haunted him, silent, head bowed over her needle, while he failed to give her the sustenance of a kind remark or gesture of affection. She seemed to ward him off, to want nothing more than a half-life, not bothering with friends or family, avoiding all emotion. He had longed, on such occasions, to shout, 'Wake up, we are fading, shrinking, becoming invisible!' But Mariella would not have understood. To erase the memory of such moments, D'Ayala said quickly, 'Would you like a television set, Alba?'

'That would be beautiful, Dottore. In colour?'

'Yes, why not? I'll see about it.'

He was as good as his word. The very next morning he stood in a hi-fi shop and found the noise intolerable, the multiplied image on the many screens like an activated Warhol painting, the whole experience bewildering as if he were being brainwashed. He was fair game for the salesman who approached him, and wrote out a large cheque without quibble.

The television set was delivered that afternoon. A young man brought it in a van, carried it single-handed up the stairs, plugged it in, twiddled knobs with panache and produced in the calm of D'Ayala's drawing-room a politician in full cry. D'Ayala winced. The young man grinned at Alba. Alba watched him pocket his tip and showed him out. D'Ayala switched the television set off with relief.

After dinner that evening, he switched it on again and Alba came to watch. The room became strangely like a place of public entertainment, loud with pop music and crowded with the jerky shadows of dancers and flashes of colour. Alba began to sway to the rhythm, swinging her hips, describing small circles with her hands. She closed her eyes, hummed a little. She began to turn, slowly, her knees slightly bent, her eyebrows raised, a little smile around her mouth. 'Alba,' said D'Ayala all of a sudden, 'you dance like an angel. Be one for me. Take off your clothes.'

Alba danced on with her eyes still closed, and D'Ayala thought that she had not heard him. Then she began to feel for the buttons of her shirt and undo them slowly, one by one. She dragged the shirt off clumsily and fast, never having seen the art of a stripper. She opened her eyes to discard the jeans, balancing awkwardly on one foot and then the other. She kicked her sandals into a corner of the room, out of her way. Resuming the dance, she wriggled out of the underclothes supplied by the nuns. At last she was naked. D'Ayala watched her with half-closed eyes and was surprised at the strength of his libido.

The programme and the music ended. Alba gathered up her clothes and calmly put them on again, watching the television as she fastened buttons and felt her way into her sandals.

Next evening D'Ayala did not need to ask Alba for her favours. As soon as she had cleared away the evening meal, she herself switched on the television, found music that pleased her, and undressed. From then on Alba danced for D'Ayala on every evening that television provided music to her liking.

D'Ayala, watching Alba, longed to touch her, just to feel a curve or press his fingers lightly round her breast, just to hold a buttock in his hand for a fleeting moment, just to stroke a thigh. But he knew that he never would permit himself such luxuries. In the last years of his marriage there had been no sex. Mariella had lost interest and he had found it easier than expected to give up the remnants of that everyday solace. The idea of approaching a young girl now with an offer of passion terrified him: he was certain that he could only disappoint her and make a fool of himself. The first touch, therefore, was the one to avoid.

Alba herself did not encourage him. She seemed content just to dance naked for him as if he were no more than an impotent old man in her eyes. When he saw himself naked in a mirror, he feared she was right.

The idea of persuading Alba to accept his caresses appalled him. His greatest horror, in dreams awake or asleep, was to hear her say, 'Don't touch me, go away, leave me alone.'

And so it was that D'Ayala, who all his life had despised the idea of voyeurism, found that he was, regularly and in his own drawing-room, a devotee of the practice.

Chapter 8

The framemaker from Agrigento approached the Institute of Fine Arts through the streets of Palermo, driving his Fiat at a cringing ten kph. When he arrived, he forced the car to judder up on to the pavement, and there he sat, waiting for his nerves to settle. Palermitan drivers are devils.

The framemaker had come to see the Director of the Institute. Some months earlier the Director had commissioned a new frame for a painting by Vasta that hung in a small church not far from Agrigento, the original frame now being more wormhole than wood. The framemaker had bought what he needed for the job, and looked forward to earning a substantial sum. Now, however, the work was cancelled. No adequate explanation had been given for the cancellation, and the framemaker was anxious to find out if the decision could be reversed. He doubted it, but he was desperate for work and was ready to make great efforts to get it.

He walked through the dim entrance of the Institute and made for the Director's office. The door was open and the Director was out, but Annamaria Schindt, at the filing cabinets, was as unhelpful as she could be. She didn't want this bumpkin from the provinces hanging about, grumbling and making trouble. He was already sounding aggressive.

'I'll go and see the Archivist,' he said. 'He knows me, he'll speak to the Director for me. He'll put things right.'

'See who you want, I don't care. But unless you have the Director's favour, you won't get anywhere. And next time you want to see him, write a letter first. He hasn't time to see all and sundry,' said Annamaria Schindt.

The framemaker intended to approach D'Ayala's office unnoticed because nobody, after all, wants to hear a complaint and for what other reason would a man drive from Agrigento? But the Institute itself was not on his side. Its ceilings were high, the corridor floors were stone, and everybody who walked about there sounded like a man of authority.

Although he heard the approaching footsteps in the corridor, D'Ayala didn't move from his desk at the window of his dusty office. Outside the window figleaves like green hands patterned his view of the sky – that high Palermitan sky he loved – and suggested coolness no matter how high the temperature rose. A large insect flew in, changed its mind, flew out again noisily. The framemaker was not as confident as the insect: he knocked softly on the doorframe and entered with cautious steps murmuring a soothing prayer, 'Dottore, how are you? I'm glad to find you here, a friendly face, a scholar's mind, a personage. . . .'

D'Ayala stood up slowly and offered his hand. 'Signor Gario, I'm glad you have called. Fetch that chair, make yourself at home. It's very hot, really it is.'

The framemaker sat at D'Ayala's elbow, leaning forward, speaking urgently now, recounting a long litany of the new Director's sins, his broken promises, his lack of understanding, his inadequate explanations to a man who had spent money on the expectations he had inspired. D'Ayala appeared to be listening. 'A new frame for the Vasta . . . .' he murmured. 'Yes, I remember now. . . .' But D'Ayala needed a very different kind of frame. A frame for Alba's dancing. A musical prelude? And postlude? Splendid, but unobtainable. Applause recorded by some great audience at the Scala, the Met, Covent Garden? Too impersonal, and technically out of reach. Curtains that could be swished open and closed, as if the drawing-room had become a private miniature theatre? Imagine the speculation they would give rise to, especially on the part of visitors such as Leila Bragazzi. But there was something in the idea of cloth, beautiful draped cloth. Yes, of course. Into D'Ayala's mind floated a vision of a gown that would hide the rough start and finish of Alba's performance, just as a frame hides nails and stretchers. No more graceless movements as she undressed, no more clothes scattered on the floor. Alba would come from her room naked except for this gown from which she would emerge, if not like Venus, then at least with all the natural allure of a flirty eighteen-year-old. When she had finished dancing, D'Ayala himself might be permitted to wrap the garment round her shoulders while whispering admiration.

The framemaker had become silent and puzzled. 'Dottore,' he said at last, 'you're a man of refinement. You know my work. Talk to the Director for me, please.'

'I'll see the Director as soon as he comes in,' said D'Ayala, feeling guilty about his lack of attention. 'The Vasta deserves a fine frame and you are the right man to make it. Leave everything to me.'

The framemaker went back to his car. For the life of him he couldn't make out what had happened during that encounter, but he felt it had done him little good.

Chapter 9

Mariella had always kept her needlework in a large chest in her bedroom. D'Ayala lifted the lid and at once felt guilty of trespass. This had been purely Mariella's domain, containing her small ambitions and satisfactions, her taste and judgement, and in every stitch she had worked were care and concentration of the first order. The chest gave forth a fragrance, the living, personal fragrance of Mariella's hands, stimulating memories so vividly that D'Ayala resolved never to open that chest again. First, however, he had to find something in it.

He pushed aside skeins of silk and wool, rolls of printed canvas stiffened until the edges threatened to cut one's fingers, sections of wooden frames, and at the very bottom of the chest came to long packages of material wrapped in yellowing tissue paper. He lifted a few of these out and tore open a small hole at the end of each to see what was inside. One of them contained a heavy white cloth which he thought might well make Alba's dancing gown.

He stood up and tore away all the wrapping and unrolled the material to its full length. Ah, but this made none of those crisp pleats and folds that would show off Alba's body like the gown on the Serpolta woman at Alcamo. This stuff formed no static shapes. This was satin and it slithered about as if it were alive. Holding the end of the piece in one hand, he flung the bulk of it out in front of him and watched it drop to the floor where it snaked into folds, one upon another. Exciting.

In the late afternoon he set out for the home of Mariella's dressmaker, taking the satin with him and making his way through noisy, narrow streets crowded with shoppers and walking carefully to avoid the droppings of horse and dog, and rubbish from a nearby market. Blessings came his way from a small shrine on a corner illuminated with electric candles; beneath it were paper flowers of a violent red. Kaplan came to mind: he would have described their colour as 'a fist to the eyeball'. Caged birds twittered above, outside windows from which radios bawled. D'Ayala enjoyed a sense of life that he hadn't felt in his own home for a long time, and he arrived earlier than he had anticipated.

The dressmaker's house was old and shabby and D'Ayala remembered that once he had collected some shirts here when his monogram had been embroidered on them. He hadn't gone inside the building, of which the dressmaker occupied part of the third floor. She had let down a basket with the work in it on the end of a rope, and from a note inside he had known how much money to put in before the basket was hauled up again.

On this day, however, he wanted to see the dressmaker in person, so he went into the building past bicycles and pram wheels at the bottom of the stairs, and climbed up in the dim light shed by a weak bulb all day long. When he reached what he thought must be her door, he knocked.

The dressmaker was nonplussed to find D'Ayala on her doorstep. Hers was a woman's world visited by lady clients only if necessary, and by men never. She put her hands nervously to her head and rammed home a straying hairpin.

'Dottore D'Ayala,' she said, 'I wasn't expecting you ... I had no idea ... I would have come to your house if you had sent for me.'

There was nothing for it but to usher him in. He stood just inside the door and felt that he could hardly breathe. The room was large, but with a small window and a low ceiling under which the smells of thousands of meals were trapped, mingled with those of sweat and old age. In the centre of the room was a table covered with pieces of paper patterns, fabric, out-of-date fashion magazines and an ancient hand-operated Singer sewing-machine. D'Ayala wondered how anybody could work in the dim light, the claustrophobic atmosphere, cavelike, oppressively smelly.

On the far side of the room, right beside the small window, sat the dressmaker's mother who did the embroidery. Did she ever leave that chair, that spot of daylight? She seemed to be part of the room's structure.

'Ah, we miss Signora D'Ayala, don't we, Mama?' bellowed the dressmaker across the room. 'My mother's deaf now, Dottore.' Not wanting to spoil the chance of a little work, she added, 'But she can see better than I can. For embroidery there's still no one to match her.'

D'Ayala could hardly believe that his embroidered shirts and Mariella's fresh summer dresses came from this stinking dungeon. He tried to imagine a fitting, with an accompaniment of flattery through a mouthful of pins. He wondered how Mariella had stood the airlessness, the suffocating attitude, the endless placating.

'Signora,' he said, pulling himself together, 'I want to give my daughter-in-law in Milan a special present because she's been so good to me since my wife died. Could you make her a negligee from this cloth I found among my wife's things?' He undid the parcel and laid the satin on the sewing table. The dressmaker rubbed the edge of the material between her fingers, lifted a corner, shook it gently. 'It'll make up beautifully,' she said with a touch of envy. 'What style had you in mind, Dottore?'

'Simple, tailored. Yes, tailored, with a long girdle. And two breast pockets.'

'And the size?'

'She's about your size. Perhaps a little taller. And one more detail – I'd like embroidery on the pockets.'

'Mother will do that, Dottore. What motif would look nice, do you think?'

D'Ayala took from his pocket a scrap of paper on which he had drawn a rosebud, face on, surrounded by a circle.

'This is the decoration on my daughter-in-law's hairbrushes,' he said, 'all in deep pink. Could your mother copy it for me in that colour?'

The dressmaker turned towards her mother and bawled, 'The Dottore's brought us both a nice bit of work.' The old woman stared, silent and motionless.

'I'll bring it round when it's ready, Dottore,' said the dressmaker. 'No need for you to come back up here.'

Two weeks later the gown was delivered to D'Ayala's apartment in a cloud of tissue paper. D'Ayala watched Alba undo it, lift it high into the air, shake it out, and hold it against herself. The two rosebuds on the pockets resembled nipples, each encircled by an aureole. Alba giggled and went to try on this new marvel. D'Ayala was glad to see her enjoying herself. He switched on the television and found himself lucky: there was music of Alba's favourite kind.

Waiting for Alba to return, D'Ayala dreamed of the garment he would have liked for himself on occasions such as this. It was a pair of Turkish trousers in Venetian red, cut from the same kind of gleaming satin as Alba's gown. As Alba danced, he could have looked down and observed, first, gentle hillocks in the satin, followed by steepening slopes, and finally by a full, upright manifestation with folds of satin spreading from it on all sides like flags of victory.

Alas, he would never own such a garment. From whom could he order something so outlandish? At the sound of it his tailor would be filled, not with imagination and romantic zeal, but with vulgar curiosity. And worse: mirth.

At that moment Alba appeared in the white gown with embroidered nipples and a haughty smile on her face. She twirled slowly to the music, letting the gown fall open at her thighs and form a short train on the floor behind her and with her fingers she made long stroking motions from her shoulders down over the embroidered nipples, the waist, and finally the hips. When she stopped, she lifted the gown back from her shoulders and dropped it. Down it slid touching every inch of her until it was on the floor, gleaming, round her feet. D'Ayala clapped softly and smiled.

Chapter 10

The Director of the Institute sat behind his desk as if he were enthroned.

'Well, Dottore, I've been meaning to have a little talk with you for some time,' he began. 'And now Rome has forced my hand. They feel that the Institute is due for some modernisation, restructuring, technical updating to simplify the work. And the place to start, of course, is in the archives. Microphotography would solve so many of our problems, I'm sure you'll agree. But the changeover means a great deal of extra work, and I hardly like to ask you to agree to such upheaval. In fact, if it were not for Rome, I wouldn't do so. But you know what they're like. I can't refuse them. Not any more.'

'You mean you've done so in the past?' This was incredible.

'Dottore, let me be frank. Rome has suggested several times that I find a young man to take over this specialist work, and I've always answered that you are indispensible. There's much more to your work than mere records – people, connections. We couldn't do without you. On the other hand, we couldn't afford to employ two archivists. Rome knew that. They considered the matter very thoroughly over a long period, and wondered if you would consider early retirement. I objected strongly. But now... well, they're insisting on some rationalisation of the matter.'

'You've taken me by surprise, Director,' said D'Ayala truthfully.

'With much regret, Dottore. But what am I to do? You will have to attend a course, naturally, to learn the techniques of processing. A few months, if you take to it easily.'

'And if I retire instead?'

'Then Rome would send you a handsome sum of money and begin paying your pension at once. Exactly how long is it since you joined the Institute?'

'My whole life back,' said D'Ayala, stunned.

'Fetch the Dottore's file,' said the Director to Annamaria Schindt. Instantly she put it before him. He pulled his calculator towards him and began to touch numbers, murmuring as he did so. His fingernails clicked on the keys.

D'Ayala fled into wild fantasy. He imagined himself in the basement of the Institute, watching, unseen, the antics of the Director and Annamaria Schindt. They were on the stone floor, she on her back, fully dressed, and the Director on top of her, naked and hairy. Her clothes began to dissolve, fuse, and finally harden into the black, shiny carapace of a beetle. Her legs sprouted claws, her every movement made a click like the Director's fingernails on the calculator. And now the Director in the basement raises his naked buttocks, thrusts strongly forward and down, and yelps as he meets that carapace. Click! Click! Yelp!

'Dottore, are you all right?' asked the Director.

'Perfectly, thank you. I was just dreaming for a moment while you made your calculations.'

'Here you are, then. It's a princely sum. Look.'

The Director pushed a slip of paper across his desk with a figure on it, insinuating that he didn't wish his secretary to be privy to such matters. D'Ayala looked at the paper and said nothing. A figure in abstract, it seemed to him.

'Plus, of course, your full pension. We are all indebted to you for your contributions to the prestige of the Institute and. . . .'

'When would I have to go?' asked D'Ayala.

'Dottore, don't think of it as "having to go". This is honourable retirement. In about a month's time, I thought. That would give you time to finish up any work you have in hand.'

So it had all been decided long before he came into the room, and he was fired.

'I suppose I can't refuse.'

The Director sighed. 'You could go to Rome and talk to them yourself, I suppose. Persuade them to support the old work methods.'

'Absurd,' said D'Ayala.

'Or you could try the training course. Why not, after all?'

'Ludicrous.'

There was silence. The Director closed D'Ayala's file and Annamaria Schindt took it from his desk and put it on a side table.

D'Ayala said slowly, 'I haven't any choice. I shall go in a month.' He rose and left the room.

As soon as D'Ayala had closed the door behind him, the Director said, 'He swallowed the lot,' and leaned back, satisfied, in his chair. Annamaria Schindt smiled slyly but said nothing. Suddenly the Director grabbed her and pulled her on to his lap, and one of his hands reached under her skirt but her thin thighs flew together so that her knees clamped his arm like a vice. In the small space left between her thigh and his stomach, a swelling appeared. Alert, she saw it. With enquiring fingers she examined it, softly. Then she drew back her hand, closed it into a hard fist, and gave a fierce jab downwards.

Chapter 11

When D'Ayala left the office of the Director of the Institute, he did not go back to his desk. Instead, he walked straight out of the Institute and down to the docks.

A boat from Ustica had just tied up and huntsmen were coming ashore, talking and laughing together, with their gundogs on the ends of tattered ropes. The dogs twisted their thin bodies, turning towards D'Ayala as if they sensed his distress and relished it; some curled their top lip in an evil grin, others barked mockingly. When the last of them had gone, the quay was quiet and D'Ayala turned his back to the sea, spread his arms wide, and in his heart addressed Palermo and all Sicily.

'I am finished,' he said. 'I shall serve you no longer.' Softly, as if in the far distance, a sound began that compelled him to listen. It was a chorus of smart-alec voices and scornful giggles that came weaving through the palms, rustling papyrus, blowing along old streets, haunting temples, whirling the dust from tesserae, flying from dome to cupola saying, 'No more! No more D'Ayala. Enough of him, he's done. Ha ha ha ha. . . .'

'Stop!' shouted D'Ayala.

Deeper voices came from Monreale, from caves and prisons, catacombs and castles, calling, 'You may go, D'Ayala. It makes no difference to us. Some other fool will take your place.'

'But I've loved and revered you all my life! Surely there must be some link between us?'

'Bits of paper, D'Ayala, just bits of paper.'

'No, there's more than that. Facts, theories, history....'

'Worthless. We are what we are and *basta*. We have no souls, no feelings, no brains, no blood, no need for Institutes, and still less for archivists.'

'But my work, my lifetime....'

'Oh,' sighed a final voice, 'go away, D'Ayala, you plead like a castrato.'

Heat shimmered as if the quay itself was melting. The sea, still and pale, blended on the horizon with a hot yellow sky. D'Ayala yearned for Alba and the cool of his shuttered apartment. He began to walk home.

Via Mabuse felt like a ravine in some desert. Even the stray cats were hiding from the sun. D'Ayala fumbled, trying to open his front door too quickly. Once inside, he took a deep cool breath and called Alba.

There was no reply, but he heard whispering from his bedroom and he opened the door and looked in. His bed was undisturbed, but two faces peered at him from over the far edge of it, the faces of Alba and the young television man. They rose, naked.

'Dottore, we didn't expect you home,' said Alba, 'and you look terrible. Rest on the bed while I go and make you some coffee.'

She left the room with perfect composure, and the young man trotted after her with his hands over his genitals. Sitting on the edge of his bed, D'Ayala could see their clothes on his bathroom floor, dropped there in the haste of desire.

When Alba came back into the bedroom, dressed and carrying the coffee, she found D'Ayala lying on his bed with his arm across his eyes. She put down the coffee on a bedside table, sat down on the bed, and leaned over him saying, 'Dottore, don't be angry with me.'

'I'm not, Alba.'

'It was nothing, Dottore. He's just the boy from the television shop, he doesn't belong here with us, and he's gone. I threw him out.'

'Alba, don't leave me. Not yet.'
'Dottore, how could you think such a thing?'
'Alba, today I lost my job. I, too, was thrown out.'
'But they can't do that, Dottore, not to you. A person like you can't be fired.'
'They can, Alba, and they have. It's a dark day today.'

Chapter 12

In the days that followed, D'Ayala altered visibly. His face sagged, giving him the expression of a different personality, and his eyes stared out overbright. His grey hair, normally well disciplined, lost its spring and hung lank and untidy. Every time he caught sight of himself in a looking-glass or shop window, he was dismayed.

But still more painful was the seeming change in his character. He became sullen, taciturn, hostile, all signs of a painful inner state. Every morning he awoke to a sense of menace that gripped the pit of his stomach so that he was nauseated, and although this passed as the day proceeded, it left a chill inner void. Externally he felt surrounded by a kind of thick glass wall that separated him from time, events, and particularly from people. Through this wall he could see them mouthing words but somehow, try as he might, he couldn't absorb the meaning, and when he himself wanted to speak to someone he had to penetrate the wall with words, words he couldn't always find, words for which he offered poor substitutes hardly worth enunciating, much less arranging in syntactical order. When he did speak, it was in a whisper.

D'Ayala's colleagues at the Institute thought the shock of his dismissal had brought about his condition. Alba put it down to anger: he had, after all, caught her in his own bedroom with the television man who was young and sure to be virile. Yet she felt it was a strange anger. She was accustomed to shouting and swearing at home and in the streets and to the voices of furious nuns boiling with rage or icy with sarcasm. D'Ayala's miserable silence she found hardest to bear, and she tried to right the situation.

'Dottore, don't be angry, I implore you. Talk to me a little. That stupid boy from the television shop is nobody. Don't be angry, Dottore.'

'I'm not angry, Alba. To tell you the truth, I don't know what is the matter with me. Perhaps I'm falling ill.'

Alba studied him but saw no signs of illness. To her, illness meant coughing or spewing or shitting, and none of these afflicted D'Ayala. Superstitions from her childhood crept into her mind and cautiously she put one hand behind her back, made it into a fist, extended the index and little fingers like horns, and jabbed them into the air to ward off the evil eye. This done, she waited hopefully for some improvement.

D'Ayala, wandering about the apartment in his dressing-gown, felt that his work might anchor him to reality in this fearful sea of dark sensations. He began to plan a short paper on a topic that had interested him for some time. It was almost impossible to concentrate, but he remembered a good many facts concerning the connection between documents long held in the archives of the Institute and one brought to light recently by the death of a land agent whose family had guarded their private papers from Sicily's many vicissitudes, including the Allied Invasion. Writing about all this, he might forget to be afraid.

So he went, one morning, to the Institute to get the appropriate documents from files in the basement. He was, after all, still the official archivist, although only for a few days more. He managed to avoid the Director, Annamaria Schindt, and most of his colleagues and descended to the cool semi-dark, the setting for his fantasy about the Director's love-life.

There were the files he knew so well. There was the drawer in which he would find all the papers he needed. He pulled it open and stood for a moment resting his hands on the tops of the crowded documents. Suddenly he shivered and felt as if

55

he were waking up, and he was aware, by instinct, that a lot of time had passed since he opened that drawer, time during which he must have stood there inert. Minutes, perhaps hours. Confused and embarrassed, he grabbed a whole section of the files and hurried upstairs with it to his office, wondering if anybody had seen him in the basement and what they had thought of him standing there. But the clock in his office was reassuring. The blank time in the basement had been merely minutes.

Nonetheless, D'Ayala was afraid and decided to go home at once. He crammed the documents into his briefcase, and left.

At home in his study, after a siesta and coffee, he took out the papers and began to read, jotting down on a pad beside him odd words, a medley of quotations, questions, cross references that came to mind and should be investigated. When he finished he read the jottings: they were total nonsense.

Tears rolled down D'Ayala's cheeks. He dribbled slightly since the muscles in his lips and chin seemed to have ceased working. Inside his head he found an alter ego into which he stepped and through whose eyes he could watch his weeping self with detachment.

Alba found him in this state.

'It's all right, Alba,' he blurted out, 'I'm not sad, and nothing hurts. In fact I don't know why I'm crying. I must look awfully silly. Take no notice.'

Alba decided that the only way to handle this bizarre situation was to take him at his word. She fetched him a clean handkerchief and went back to the kitchen to get on with her work, but she worried and never behaved so coolly again.

This sideways move into the alter ego was short, but it happened again and again, each time giving him brief respite. However, he did not return to the Institute because he could not control the weeping, which became more and more frequent and was not always accompanied by the escape into the alter ego.

Leila Bragazzi came to call one day and found him at his worst. She recommended camomile tea and went away reflecting that her father had been quite right: D'Ayala was namby-pamby. As for the new maid, she was nothing but a slut. Thank God Mariella could not see her home these days.

Alba mothered D'Ayala. She sat with him, stroking his hair. She led him to the dinner table and helped him to eat. She talked all the time, soothingly, as to a child in trouble, and her patience was immense. She didn't give up until the day she found him on his bed, unable to move or speak at all; then she went to the telephone, found Paolo's number in Milan, and rang him.

After the 'phone call she went to her room and packed her suitcase. The dress that the nuns had given her she threw away. The dance gown she folded with care and arranged on the top of her few belongings, and when she had finished she went to D'Ayala's room and sat with him waiting for time to pass and night to fall.

At last the brief dusk of the south became apparent through the windows and Alba knew that her vigil was nearly ended. Paolo had talked of an evening plane: she had impressed him with the urgency of the situation.

The sky was dark purple when the headlights of a car shone through the window, lighting D'Ayala's room for an instant and then fanning down the wall. Alba heard the car stop, heard the clench of brakes. D'Ayala did not move. Alba got quickly to her feet, kissed his cheek, and went out into the hall. Her suitcase was ready, she had only to pick it up and let herself out of the apartment. Hiding beneath the stairs she heard Paolo and Laura going up, opening the front door, irritated and anxious, calling her name, calling D'Ayala. Quietly she stole out of the front door and away down the street.

Chapter 13

D'Ayala travelled with Paolo and Laura to Milan by air. It was not so much a journey as a displacement.

The true journey from Palermo, in D'Ayala's opinion, began with a night crossing from Palermo to Naples on a ship of the Tyrrhenian Line in unchanging turn-of-the-century comfort. Panelled staterooms, potted palms on long red carpets, first-rate service in the dining-saloon – these were still the hallmarks of that voyage. They were followed by a proper approach to the mainland in early morning, sailing into the Bay of Naples while the air was still cool, almost chilly, but the sunshine brilliant and reassuring. Vesuvius, at that hour, had the aspect of an eternal, approving mother.

In Naples D'Ayala would take a taxi to the railway station and there board a train of quite another generation; upholstered in pale blue velvet, with soothing music and press-button luxuries, it stood ready to speed north in air-conditioned near-silence. Its technological wonders enhanced D'Ayala's view of modern Italy, flat or hilly, bleak or garlanded with vines, tempting, wayward, gorgeous. After such a journey, he arrived in Milan feeling that he had experienced distance, revitalised old contacts as he did so, and exposed his imagination to fresh kindling. To fly was a hollow passing of time.

On this occasion, however, he did not mind. Through layers of depression he had sunk too deep.

Chapter 14

'You're not going to believe this,' said the man in white at the far side of the desk, 'but in three weeks you won't know yourself. All of a sudden you'll feel perfectly normal again.'

D'Ayala was slouched in a chrome and leather chair with an eye-level view of the desk top. The pages of the doctor's diary made two low cliffs separated by metal rings that suggested contemporary sculpture. The ends of pencils and ballpoints emerged obliquely from a plastic pot like a miniature industrial chimney. Papers were imprisoned in a wire basket. Two telephones threw shadows on to the white formica surface of the desk, a surface scarred with fine scratches. Someone had scoured that formica with an abrasive cleaner many times. What did the cleaner wish to remove? The tears and lies and pitiful threats of the mentally ill?

The doctor was a psychiatrist named Rossi, still in his early thirties and already a star. He wore a thick black beard to resemble both Christ and Freud, but his hands were young and free of wrinkles and other signs of hard work. His mind, however, had slogged its way to the top of the tree: several of his papers had been accepted by psychiatric journals, and he was at the peak of preparation for the highest available qualification in his chosen field. He saw his future spent chairing committees where he would be heard and applauded.

The net result was confidence calm and deep as a well, and he would spread a little of it over his patients, brightening them up as with a coat of aspic.

D'Ayala, however, had doubts. He saw Dr Rossi as a whippersnapper condescending to his elders. How could such a fellow, young enough to be one's son, know much about life in general? Through what personal crises had he lived? Looking back over his short span of life, how much cause could he have for regret? Here he came again with more idiot questions.

'And don't you feel better now that you're with your family, Dottore D'Ayala?' Better, worse, who could tell? D'Ayala had no idea how he was, confusion being a major ingredient of his state of mind.

'Tell me about sleeping,' went on Dr Rossi, attentively and without understanding. 'How do you sleep? Do you dream much?'

D'Ayala wondered if he could define sleep nowadays. Was it sitting open-eyed, lost in time? Or waiting, for who knows what? Or watching a crack in the floor for minutes, perhaps hours, not expecting anything to happen to the crack, but compelled to watch it, nonetheless? As for dreams, as soon as D'Ayala was in bed he fell into a black hole, and there witnessed horrifying sequences against which nobody in the dreams protested and he himself was powerless to react. He had once seen the head of a donkey lying on its side, strapped to wheels which enabled it to be moved around as it grazed. Its neck, body, legs, and entrails had been blown off in an explosion, he was told by strangers with matter-of-fact voices. He longed to awake, and when he did so it was always far too early in the morning and doom came down over him like a bell cloche.

But one must try to say something to the doctor for the sake of politeness. D'Ayala leaned forward until his chin was almost on the desk. He ran his thumbnail along one of the scratches in the formica, following it with great care as tears dripped from his face and splashed down. He couldn't speak.

'Modern drugs work wonders,' said the doctor, 'and there's no need to soldier on these days. As I said, you won't know yourself. Just be patient. And now, why don't you go and wait in the Day Room while I have a word with your daughter-in-law?'

The Day Room was peopled with figures who did not communicate, and sat still on red and yellow plastic chairs staring ahead or down at the floor. Some dribbled. D'Ayala sat down next to a woman who had smeared her face with dollops of make-up. Suddenly she gave a shout, but nobody took any notice. A young man on the far side of the room rose and climbed up on to a table, where he sang a mediaeval French song with remarkable skill and beauty: yet not a face turned towards him, not even after a note, a phrase, a verse. When he had finished he climbed down again and resumed his seat. D'Ayala would have liked to applaud, but the effort was too great.

After some time a nurse came to the Day Room and looked round. 'Ah, there you are, Dottore D'Ayala. Come along now, your daughter-in-law is waiting for you. Let's go to the car.' She took D'Ayala's arm and guided him firmly in the direction she wanted him to go.

On the way home Laura said, 'You'll have to do just what Dr Rossi said, you know. Take the tablets and wait.' She looked at D'Ayala out of the corner of her eye. He was studying his lap, and inexplicably she felt guilty. To relieve her guilt, she slammed the gear lever into third and drove up to the Condominium garages with plenty of noise, yanking on the handbrake when they stopped as if she was punishing it. They got out into the middle of a crowd of children on rollerskates and women who had been shopping.

'Laura, *ciao*! Where've you been?'

'Tennis tomorrow, Laura?'

'Is this your father-in-law?'

'Did you take him to the clinic, Laura, to Dr Rossi?'

'Rossi's marvellous . . . when my mother-in-law went ga-ga. . . .'

'Lithium, of course. . . .'

'Oh no, not lithium, the side-effects are awful . . . poor thing, doesn't he look terrible. . . .'

D'Ayala touched Laura's arm. 'Take me upstairs,' he begged.

Two children came by, screaming and grabbing at each other as they tried to keep their balance on the rollerskates. Instantly D'Ayala knew to what the donkey's head had been attached, and he cringed.

'Idiots!' screamed Laura at the children. 'Get away from here! Do you want to knock somebody down?' She seized D'Ayala by the arm and drew him towards her, safely away from the rollerskates. It was the first time she had ever had to protect him, and when she looked at him and saw how the depression had pulled down his face and even altered his posture so that he looked bent and old, she was appalled. Of all her husband's family, Lorenzo D'Ayala had always pleased her most, looking so tall and well-bred and dressing with such subtle taste that it was a joy to walk with him and be seen in any fashionable place. Now she wanted to hide him. She pushed him into the building and took him up to the flat.

Thereafter, for some time, D'Ayala stayed in the flat. He didn't want company: the glass wall in front of his mind was too thick and disabling. All that he noticed through it were the manoeuvres of his family as they tried to avoid spending much time with him. His grandson held up schoolbooks and said, smiling, 'Homework, Grandpa. They give us so much we're never free of it.' Paolo, coming home from his office, rushed in to say, 'How are you, Father? You look much better. I've just got to make a 'phone call. . . .'

Laura appeared more often, bringing him his pills or fetching him to table for a meal. He was grateful to her and hoped that Dr Rossi's prognosis was right. For whatever happened, D'Ayala knew that he was not going to stay in Milan.

He spent his days wandering about the flat, sleeping at odd hours and awaking confused, and sitting. He sat most of all in an armchair in the sitting-room window where he had a good view of the Condominium's landscape, a scene that exactly matched his fragmented thoughts and sense of lost identity. Fields of thin grass surrounded the Condominium, awaiting the giant hand and purse of the developer, and they were dotted with small, shoddy factories producing gimcrackery for the Common Market. Above each factory was its name in lights, lights that flickered uncertainly. When one letter of the alphabet refused to light up at all, D'Ayala saw it as a bad omen for the Board Room. He had favourites among the factories, and when he saw any sign of life, such as a lorry leaving its premises, he followed its route through the narrow lanes that crisscrossed the area and led to nothing but crawling and hold-ups on half-finished roads among piles of rusty chain-link fencing and broken concrete.

The Milanese sky pressed down on that landscape. D'Ayala could feel it. The developers who had built the Condominium and, no doubt, promised a whole new deal for its surrounding countryside, had ignored the hot humid greyness that would give so many people a bad temper so often. On the other hand, the landscape made no demands on those who looked at it: there wasn't a single item of historic interest or aesthetic appeal between the Condominium and the horizon. This suited D'Ayala admirably, and he returned to it thankfully and often.

He found the kitchen bearable for short visits and ate his lunch there because it was easier for Laura on her own. He sat on a high stool and gazed around at the electric gadgetry that pulsed, whined, clicked and hummed, hurrying to get done in minutes the work that maids in Palermo had carried out in day-long rituals.

'Tablets, Father-in-law.'

D'Ayala felt that he cheated Laura sometimes by entering his alter ego. At such moments – unfortunately rare – he found himself able to trust implicitly in the medication and to be sure beyond any doubt that Dr Rossi's promise of a sudden cure was genuine. Even the tearful, doubting D'Ayala could not upset the alter ego. And seen through its eyes, the Condominium's landscape was about to receive, by some secular miracle, the beauty of Sicily.

Laura, looking at the back of D'Ayala's head as he sat at the window, wondered when she would be able to escape. The effect of the tablets was cumulative, Dr Rossi had said. Days were passing. But at the moment even a visit to the supermarket was a treat. She gathered courage and decided to ask D'Ayala straight out if he needed her constantly.

'Laura, you should go out,' he said. 'I'm fine.' He was sorry that he had put her in that supplicant's position, and surprised that the glass wall was momentarily so thin.

Laura spent an hour telephoning in her bedroom that morning, and while D'Ayala ate his lunch she told him that she was going to play tennis in the afternoon.

'You're sure you'll be all right? I shan't be far away.'

'Of course. Don't worry about me,' he said, hoping that his voice sounded confident. Inside he was stricken with fear.

As soon as she had gone he went to the kitchen to look for whisky, and as he poured himself a drink he heard Laura's voice through the kitchen window and peeped down between the slats of the blind. Laura was standing by a car below and laughing in a way he hadn't seen her laugh for years. The driver of the car, a dark man considerably younger than she, leaned over and opened the door for her.

'Come on, Pussy-cat, let's go.'

She got in, showing off her long sun-tanned legs below tennis shorts, and slammed the door shut after her. Immediately the car departed with a roar and a screech of tyres.

D'Ayala went back to the sitting-room window and watched the car as it set out into his landscape and made for Milan.

In the car, Laura leaned back and stretched herself, exulting in this temporary freedom. Under the dashboard she made little circles in the air with her feet and watched them as if she were delighting in a game played by two children. She pressed the palms of her hands together, she smiled to herself.

'Well, how does it feel to be out and about again?' asked the man at the wheel of the car. He kept his eyes on the road, but his hand felt for her thigh.

'Good. Very good,' she said.

She had been missing, painfully, her privacy at home and longed for its restitution. Before D'Ayala's arrival she had regarded the apartment, at least in daytime, as very much her own world where she could do as she wished. She had, in fact, entertained the driver of the car twice during D'Ayala's illness, but with inhibitions. D'Ayala had heard her as he shuffled to the bathroom.

'It's all right,' she was whispering. 'Don't stop.'

'Laura, kitten, he'll hear us. What if he comes down the corridor?'

D'Ayala had hurried back to the sitting-room, but not until he had heard her replying, 'He won't, really he won't. He sits there for hours on end, and if he wants me, he calls out. He's not the sort to creep about listening. When he's better, we'll have to make other arrangements.'

D'Ayala couldn't blame Laura. He could well believe that Paolo was impotent these days, yet there was Laura brimming with energy, elegantly groomed, classy, smelling beautiful, obviously feeling beautiful and, perhaps unconsciously, inviting beautiful sport. Even emerging from her bathroom she looked distinguished and appealing: she wore a white bathrobe pinched in at the waist by a girdle, and her height was emphasised by a tall white turban hiding her hair and by spike-heeled white mules from which the arches of her narrow feet rose in bony, well-defined curves. Certainly she should not settle for a half-life. It would be a wicked waste.

D'Ayala wondered, as he had from time to time, why Laura had married Paolo. She was too clever to have married for love, romance or sex. There must have been other factors. Security was probably one of them. Paolo had never been hard up, nor had he seemed to be hard up, even as a student, and, however much he might flounder in the business world, he was a lawyer with formal legal qualifications that were bound to be useful and were socially acceptable. The D'Ayala name itself had a certain value. And – D'Ayala enjoyed a wicked thought – Laura did not disdain her father-in-law for any reason. He preened himself with this reflection and felt a little better.

He did not know, however, that Laura was already taking practical steps towards a satisfactory arrangement of her future. She had heard of a small flat standing empty at the far side of the Condominium and had made enquiries about its purchase for her father-in-law. She was determined that he should take it. If he had known that she had passed that very morning wandering round it, pencil and paper in hand, trying to visualise the Palermitan furniture confined in these shoe-box rooms, he would have been alarmed.

'I'll have to bring in only the smallest things,' said Laura to herself. 'The rest of the furniture will have to go. And so will those silk shirts. I'll never get anyone to iron them these days.'

Chapter 15

As if a switch had been thrown, D'Ayala's depression lifted. The wall of glass was gone. The sensation of menace was instantly replaced by optimism. Although he felt physically weak and tired, he knew he was well again.

He looked round the dinner table at which his family sat, eating in businesslike silence.

'I think I'm better,' he said.

'Good. Fine,' said Paolo without looking up.

'No, no, I mean it. All of a sudden I'm well. I feel myself again.'

This time Paolo looked at him and Laura put down her fork and stared. 'Good God,' she said, 'Dr Rossi was right. I thought he was exaggerating at the time.'

D'Ayala seemed to see them properly at last, Laura bolt upright, dominating the table, her eyebrows raised, her long face full of amazement, while Paolo, puffy and middle-aged, frowned in bewilderment and disbelief. The grandson looked alarmed: he had been afraid of his sick grandfather and didn't know what to make of the well one. They were all on the defensive.

'You mustn't worry about me now. I can think clearly again. I'm sorry I've been such a nuisance.'

They mumbled polite denials and got on with their meal to

hide their perplexity. When it was over, D'Ayala said, 'I think I'll go for a short walk. Just a little stroll. It's a long time since I was outside.'

'Paolo will go with you,' said Laura. 'You're bound to be weak and you'll have to be careful.'

As they emerged from the lift on the ground floor, Paolo took his father's arm. D'Ayala didn't need the support, but the gesture was so pleasant that he accepted it. Every detail of his experience, minute by minute, second by second, was impressing itself upon him with extraordinary clarity.

Together father and son crossed the hall and stepped out on to the black marble entrance step, grandiose as the doorstep of a mausoleum but teased by nature. Wispy grass was growing at its edges, leaning towards the doorway as if trying to get in. Outside was a path of cracked concrete, laid ten years before as a temporary solution to the mud, but now the mud oozed up where it could and grass and weeds came with it, fighting their way towards the light.

'The builders promise every year to do this path,' grumbled Paolo, 'but they never do. One day I shall trip on it and break an ankle. I don't know what I pay service and maintenance for.'

He and his father walked to the end of the path and a short way down the lane that ran past the Condominium. The sky above them leaned low and heavy, but it couldn't crush D'Ayala's spirits. The little factories flashed and flickered.

'I know this landscape well,' said D'Ayala, 'and we've come far enough for today.'

As they walked slowly back, Paolo said, 'You should take a flat in the Condominium, Father. Laura and I both think that's the best plan. Palermo is out of the question now.'

D'Ayala was silent. Throughout his depression, time had been disordered, days had melted one into another without definition, hours had become short and long simultaneously, minutes had sometimes stopped in mid-passage and resumed their momentum very late. In this temporal muddle, D'Ayala could not look ahead at all, not even hours ahead. He had, therefore, taken to living for the present moment. He simply could not imagine plans for his future, and when he heard Paolo's suggestion, he was alarmed.

'Listen,' he said, 'I really can't think about anything like that just yet. I've only just woken up, as it were.'

'Yes, I suppose so,' said Paolo, annoyed that even his own father was proving uncooperative.

During the next few days D'Ayala frequently nudged his mind with the thought, 'I'm better, I'm weak but I'm well, I am myself again.' It was so exciting, this revelation; he felt like a child who has received a coveted gift at Christmas. He wandered slowly about the flat, looking, as if for the first time, at the details of its decor, the soft blond leather and steel furniture, the lamps, contorted in shape but still bare and noncommittal, the modern paintings. These last he saw with his professional eye and wondered how much they would bring at auction. Some left him unmoved, others tweaked him into life. It was gratifying to see that Paolo shared at least one of his interests.

Occasionally, feeling particularly optimistic, he set out for a walk, but his legs had weakened and wouldn't carry him far from the Condominium. He soon learned where he could sit down for a moment's rest. There was a packing case in the corner of a field, the broken axle of a lorry in a ditch beside the lane, a pile of rusting iron railings on which he could spread his newspaper before sitting down. These became his seats and observation points.

It was on his return from such a walk one day that he overheard Laura on the telephone.

'Palermo. I want Palermo. Is that Palermo? I want the number of Bragazzi. Bergamo, Roma, Anzio, Genova. . . .'

D'Ayala moved softly down the hall to hear better. He heard Laura greeting Leila, and then a quick change to businesslike tones.

'You mean that's all they said?' Laura was asking. 'I'd have thought it would fetch twice that, an apartment of that size . . . yes, of course it needs modernising . . . do try again, Leila . . . . And have you had a chance to think about the furniture? A good saleroom . . . Listen, Leila, I'll ring you again in a day or two . . . yes, I've got your number now.'

So Laura and Leila Bragazzi were selling his apartment and his belongings without so much as consulting him. Was he still so ill that he could be ignored? He leaned sideways to see himself in the hall looking glass, and saw there how pale he was and how his face still seemed to hang down, although in himself he felt quite buoyant.

'Laura misjudges me,' he said to his mirror image. 'She thinks I'm a brave liar. She doesn't realise the extent of my improvement.'

And he was afraid that, with her lists and calculations all complete, she would come to him one day and hand him a pen. 'Just sign here, Father-in-law, and I'll give you a new life.'

No, he would not sign. He wanted a new life, but not of Laura's kind. He had no idea what he should do, but he would not sign for Laura. He thought of his old furniture and wondered how much it could endure on the journey from Palermo. He imagined the squeaks and groans of old wood in the hold of a ship, the shock as the vessel bumped the quayside, the strains imposed by the movement of a train. And all for what? Everything that came from Palermo would look grotesque against the walls of a modern flat and as sad as goods up for auction. The whole business was preposterous and he longed to say, 'Dear Laura, let us sit down and discuss the possible.'

It was she herself who eventually suggested a quiet talk, but from the outset he realised that it was not to be about the new apartment. With care she avoided that subject, fearing that if it came out into the open he would – as he still could – scotch the whole idea. In a few weeks, when everything was brought near to completion, she would have him in a different position, faced with difficulties and expense if he did not comply with her plans for him.

In the meantime she needed a little time to herself, regularly and without worry, knowing that he was in the care of other people.

'Father-in-law, it's lovely to see you so much better. I'm so glad.'

He smiled nervously and was tempted to follow a crack in the wooden arm of his chair with his thumbnail. Laura's concern sounded artificial and there was an air of formal confrontation about her.

'Now don't you think it's time we found you a few friends round here, people of your own generation? We can't have you sitting on your own all day long now that you're better.'

D'Ayala felt himself shrinking back into the sick man he had been until so recently. He couldn't cope with her condescension.

'I'm sure you must miss your Palermitan friends, but they'll be glad you're here, well looked after.' She smiled, feeling generous, and then tried another tack. 'You know, the Condominium is really quite well organised – there are clubs for tennis and children and discos for the teenagers and even a club for senior residents.' She was watching him closely, ready to sooth him at once if he gave a negative signal or to boost any interest he might show.

'Geriatric get-togethers, my dear? I didn't know I had arrived,' he said with a small, twisted smile.

'Don't be difficult,' snapped Laura.

'I'm not. But the thought of joining in....'

'Bridge classes, that's all. That's how they spend most of their time. They all seem to enjoy it, so why shouldn't you?'

D'Ayala had never played cards, much to the annoyance of Leila Bragazzi who spent a great deal of time and effort making up fours. Mariella played, but badly. D'Ayala had always felt, deep in his heart, that cards were a waste of good reading time.

'Oh, I'm no good at cards. I never could take to them.'

'Not before, perhaps, when you had your work. But now?' She had toned down her voice with care.

'I'll see,' he said. It occurred to him that he had not only refused Laura's offer of an introduction to bridge classes, but also spurned the people in those classes, and he felt boorish.

'Of course I'd like to meet the people,' he said feebly.

Chapter 16

Marchesa Donata de Ferrante sat on the side of her bed, looked down at the feather-trimmed hem of her dressing-gown and swore gently, '*Accidempoli.*' The dressing-gown was very old but had miraculously kept its feathers until this day. Then, in one moment, the hem had been caught on a castor at the foot of the bed and been plucked like a chicken for several inches. The room was too small, far too small, to accommodate a human being, especially one of the Marchesa's statuesque build, and this sort of annoying incident was frequent. What next? She got up and went to the window which not even the grand curtains and pelmet she had brought from Rome could hide properly. The window frame was metal, narrow and cheap, and the view outside matched it. The Marchesa's flat looked on to the inner garden of the Condominium, on to grass seldom reached by sunshine, a dark pond with slow fish, a thin tree that wept with good reason because its roots were pressed against the footings of the surrounding walls and therefore starved and distorted. Of the sodden Milanese sky, only a patch could be seen.

The Marchesa went back to her bedside and began to dress, struggling into her corset, taking care to draw up the wrinkles from her stockings, minding the diamond rings that she never took off. When she had climbed into her dress and fastened it, she turned to the dressing table and picked up a hairbrush with a tortoiseshell back. Her hair was long, and still thick and red; she brushed it down her back over each shoulder and then piled it on top of her head with quick, sure movements and pinned it in place. Leaning forward, she peered at the mirror in semi-darkness, saw her big face and heavily hooded eyes, and pulled a face at herself.

Back to the window she went, just for a last moment before leaving the flat and meeting her public. She looked out at the far wall of the Condominium, so like a barracks. If only the architect had made the building as a whole into a positive statement of some sort. She thought of architects she had known, men of her own generation flourishing in the twenties and thirties, driven by zeal and the spirit of a new age. How full of life all her circle had been then, thrilled by speeches and rallies, crazy about anything at all new and daring.

She recalled that splendid day when she and her friends stood in a crowd on the bank of the Tiber and witnessed history in the making, the Duce signing the underside of the wing of a seaplane that floated proudly on the river all ready for the first-ever flight to Australia where, amid curious throngs, the signature would be found and verified by local officials. De Pinedo was the pilot: the Duce was embracing him, grinning with satisfaction. Ah, what an occasion! What people, all larger than life-size! And what glamour, what style! Not only were people beautiful then, but so were objects. Individual taste demanded fulfilment in everything from shoes to the handwrought carriage work of Alfa Romeos. As if in a sharp photograph she could see the custom-built open Lancia in which she and some of her crowd took a little trip one sunny day, lying back, sprawling shoulder to shoulder, thigh by thigh, watching walls of small Roman bricks and the dark undersides of umbrella pines passing slowly above them against a cerulean sky. They left the Parioli and headed for the latest marvel, Marcello Piacentini's Stadio dei Mormi. Or, to tell the truth, its grotesque statuary with outsize genitals. The car paused at a good vantage point, and somebody in the back seat crowed, 'If ever the Pope comes up here, they'll have to put knickers on these fellows!' The rest of the carload chortled with glee. Oh, it was such fun, such fun! Nobody seemed to have fun these days. Nobody seemed to have had fun, in fact, since those mad, glorious days. When she told her children about them, they assumed expressions that said 'Not funny.' Her grandchildren merely rolled their eyes heavenward. So now she had to be very careful to whom she mentioned those days, choosing only a likeminded audience, and even then she must appear to be diffident and possessed of an open mind when mention was made of special people like, say, D'Annunzio. Could it be true, she wondered, that he had had the idea of humiliating political opponents by dosing them with castor oil? Surely not. But he was, she had to admit, a carnal man, noisy and belligerent, scrawling his name in huge, savage writing on political agreements as much as on works of literature. She seemed to have had to swallow so many unpleasantnesses since then: watching such a hero evaporate before her eyes was just another of them. She knew that she was lucky still to have some capital in the bank and the lease of this mean little flat with metal window frames in a Condominium just outside Milan.

The Marchesa's daughter, who lived at the far side of the Condominium with her large family, had brought her mother, newly-widowed, to this place. 'So that I can keep an eye on you,' she had said. 'A kind of private sheltered accommodation,' said the daughter's husband, an English member of a wine shipping syndicate in Milan. The secretary of the syndicate was a fussy little man called Paolo D'Ayala whose wife had a finger in every sort of pie in the Condominium and it was she who had told the Marchesa's daughter that this small flat was available.

The Marchesa sighed. Next week she planned to take her grandchildren to Lake Garda where they would visit the house of D'Annunzio, at least, and get some idea of the splendour that she had known when she was a girl and that should rightly have been theirs today.

Meanwhile, there was bridge. Bridge and that gaggle of old women who relied on her for their entertainment and were willing to laugh at her jokes in return or shrink from her tempers like a Greek chorus. She didn't always feel like taking bridge classes, and for a moment she sank down on the bed. But then another thought occurred to her: today would be different. A man was going to join them. The father of that Paolo D'Ayala but in no way like him, she had heard. A man of some standing, a Palermitan. Palermitan? The Marchesa wondered. She had known Sicilian aristocrats in her youth, but that was no reason to suppose that this man would be any better than a retired politician of some sort. Nonetheless, to be on the safe side she put a photograph of her childhood home, an immense villa near Naples, into her handbag in case she needed its backup when establishing herself.

She rose again from the bed, patted her hair, and went to the games room of the Condominium Club ready for anything but expecting little.

The bridge class was over and D'Ayala's humiliation was complete. He was on his hands and knees under the card table, picking up cards he had dropped yet again and hiding from the ladies who had – oh, the pain of good intentions! – offered him their hands and a pull up on to his chair. They had been charming and merciless. He was the butt of their kind laughter, their flirtation, their knowing expressions, their sympathy. He watched their legs as they moved away from the table towards the bar for coffee, one or two of them bending down to smile at him under the table and ask, 'Are you coming, Professore?' He smirked back, said nothing.

But the legs of the Marchesa were still in place, her knees under the table with him, and she was, to judge by the sound of it, tapping her score pad with her pencil in agitation. She had been ruthless with him and was waiting for him to reappear. He backed out from under the table, rose to a kneeling position, and sat back on his heels looking at her.

She lowered her eyelids until they half covered her eyes and gave her a calculating expression. Then she said slowly, as if she had rehearsed the words, 'Professore, run away from here. Don't get trapped like the rest of us.'

He looked at her with astonishment.

'You're young, you can do it. Start again somewhere, I implore you. You can do better than this.' In D'Ayala she sensed the essence of men of her own generation, and she urgently wanted him to go and retrieve the lost standards and emotional certainties.

'I intend to go,' said D'Ayala, 'now that I'm better. I couldn't stay here. You're kind to have pointed it out.'

'Go back to your own style,' she said smiling, conspiratorial. But his answer surprised her.

'No, no, not back,' he said. 'I have to go forward.'

Chapter 17

A few days later Paolo, coming home from his office in the evening, stopped at the battery of mail boxes in the hall of the Condominium and found a letter addressed to his father. It had travelled far, coming from London by way of Palermo, and was smudged and readdressed and looked old although it had never been opened. Paolo took it upstairs with him.

'Good evening, Father. This is for you. A letter from London.'

'Aha,' said D'Ayala. 'At last.'

He took the letter to his chair by the window, sat down and opened it slowly. Behind him he could hear the clattering of dishes as Laura prepared dinner, and the whines and protests of his grandson, made to lay the table. But those noises, and the sight of the landscape in front of him, melted into nothing as he unfolded the letter and began to read.

Norden Nursing Home
Putney, London
10th July 1973

My dear Lorenzo,

What a pleasure it was to receive your letter. As you see, I am *hors de combat*, so to have news of an old friend is particularly sweet. We last exchanged letters, I think, when Miriam died.

I am giving up my house in Wimbledon now and hope that they will keep me here or find me a place in a residential home when I am stronger. In any case, I have to sell my paintings and I wonder if you or your Institute would be interested in any of them? Come and see – it's a marvellous excuse for visiting me!

Please give my regards to your son. And to you, my dear, may I wish bon voyage?

Kaplan

PS My son didn't want to continue the publishing business so I have sold that, too. The result should keep me comfortably all the rest of my days. K.

D'Ayala's hands holding the letter dropped to his lap and he leaned back in his chair.

'Who's the letter from, Father?' asked Paolo whose curiosity had been stirred by the English stamps.

There was a pause. Then D'Ayala said, 'It's from Kaplan. Kaplan . . . I don't think you ever knew him, did you?'

'I heard Mama speak of him . . . a publisher in London, Jewish, escaped from Vienna. . . .'

'Yes,' said D'Ayala. 'That's Kaplan. Here, I think you should read this,' and he gave the letter to Paolo.

Laura came from the kitchen, wiping her hands on a cloth and saying, 'What's going on?' She saw the letter in Paolo's hands and read it over his shoulder. When she had finished she said, 'Of course you won't be going. Just tell him you've been ill and are still far from well.'

'But I shall go,' said D'Ayala. 'That is exactly what I shall do. I can think of nothing I'd like better than a trip to London. It's ages since I was there.'

Laura took a step backward. 'That's absurd,' she said. 'What will I tell Dr Rossi? And how will you get your medication? And what will I do about the flat and Palermo and the furniture? Paolo, say something.'

Paolo, cornered, said, 'Look here, Father, I haven't time to come rushing over to London to fetch you back if you're ill again.'

'My dear children,' said D'Ayala, 'I have no intention of

being ill again, and Palermo can wait, and Dr Rossi can supply me with pills in advance. In any case, what about the famous British National Health Service? Where could I be safer?'

He was going to London, that was certain. But he knew he could never make Laura and Paolo understand that he saw the visit and the reunion with Kaplan as a chance, at last, to be a modern man, and his own.

Chapter 18

D'Ayala arrived in London on a chilly August evening and walked across the glistening tarmac to queue, as in a concentration camp, under the stern gaze of officials. The moment he had passed their high wooden desks he was a free man competing for a luggage trolley and, eventually, for a taxi. He had forgotten that the taxi would be not a sleek modern automobile but a black box in which the driver sat high up and commanded his vehicle to wend its way to its destination performing small acrobatic feats among cars and buses with a daintiness and precision that were quite surprising. D'Ayala was too excited to relax.

'This do, sir?' The taxi had stopped at the end of the Kensington street in which D'Ayala's hotel stood. 'Otherwise, I'll have to take you right round the back,' said the driver. D'Ayala got out, paid the driver, heaved his suitcase down on to the pavement. With every one of the few steps to the hotel he regretted that he had not insisted on being carried right to the door. When he arrived there was nobody in sight to give him a hand, and he approached the reception desk cross and panting and, he was sure, dishevelled.

Later he sat on the bed in his tiny room with his feet under the bedclothes for warmth and a street map spread across his knees. Here, under his fingers, were places that his mother had taken him for a treat when he was small. Here was Bloomsbury that he had known with Kaplan. Here was Wimbledon. And here was Putney. He would have to ask about buses after dinner. He dozed for a few minutes and the map slipped to the floor and awoke him, so he got up and prepared himself for dinner.

'Good evening....' 'Good evening....' Elderly couples at small tables in the dining-room downstairs looked up at D'Ayala with careful smiles. At a corner table a young man turned right round to stare, but did not speak. D'Ayala acknowledged everybody with small bows, and sat down at the first empty table he came to. While waiting for his order, he watched the elderly handle their soup-spoons and knives and forks in slow motion, as if reluctant to give way to such base business as eating. The food, when it came, was hardly worthy of their delicate approach, but they did not complain, they touched the corners of their mouths with their napkins and rose and went to the lounge to take coffee as far as possible from the kitchen.

D'Ayala ate a little with no pleasure. He got up and went to the reception desk to enquire about buses to Putney, and afterwards retired to bed. The day had been a long one.

Next morning it was raining. D'Ayala ate a huge breakfast with gusto and then, well equipped for the weather, went out to take a Putney bus. The bus ambled through wet streets, stopping frequently with a jerk as if it had been caught speeding, and set off each time with plenty of noise from the gearbox and a plaintive sound from the engine. After a long journey the Thames came into sight, adding to the watery view. The bus crawled over Putney Bridge and up the High Street and stopped at Putney Station. There a queue was waiting, anxious to get out of the wet, and as D'Ayala stepped down from the platform people surged up on to it, smelling of wet wool and creaking with plastic.

'Let 'em off first!' yelled the conductor.

D'Ayala, as soon as he was clear of the little crowd, put up his umbrella, crossed the road at the lights, and set off down Upper Richmond Road under the rain.

Rain? No, the right word was 'drizzle'. He was pleased with

himself for knowing it, and walked upright. But not for long. The drizzle didn't fall neatly from the edges of the umbrella, leaving him dry; it crept underneath, dampened his face, made his bare hand holding the handle red and cold. Little by little his shoulders hunched forward, his chin sank towards his chest, his spirits slumped. He felt as dismal as when a sudden wind from the sea rattled the palms of Palermo. But that was a brief threat: here sorrowful nature could keep on weeping for days. He heard, from long ago, his mother's voice saying, 'One misty moisty morning,' and at once he recognized this dim, grey light in which nothing was sharply defined as the very source of English poetry. He could himself people the street ahead of him with dream characters. This also accounted, to his mind, for the shortage of good English sculpture and paintings. What price visual arts in a climate where one cannot see?

He had memorised his route carefully and now turned into a side street. Here were raw brick houses that looked as if the builders had never finished them although they were already old. Some had square front windows projecting into the front garden like drawers left open. All of them had dripping, leafy surroundings that merged with trees planted in the pavement, and from not one of them came any sound of life. The strange silence haunted him. He was glad when a milk float sighed towards him and pulled up with a crunch of brakes. A dog appeared and led him, pausing at every tree, to the top of the street. There D'Ayala turned right and left the dog watching him from the corner.

In this new street was the nursing-home, and in the nursing home was Kaplan. D'Ayala walked past crescent-shaped drives and began to hope that he would not find his goal. He felt too low to face it. But the nursing home couldn't be missed. Its name was displayed in large letters on a board that stood above dank rhododendrons and camellias: 'Norden House. Private Nursing Home.' There was no going back now. D'Ayala walked up the short drive, made his way between parked cars and pressed a brass doorbell worn almost flat with polishing.

The door was opened by a young West Indian nurse whose

smile made up for the miserable weather and last-minute doubts.

'Good morning. Come right in. Who did you want to see?'
'Dr George Kaplan.'
'Oh yes. Will you wait here while I find Matron?'

The hall was large and barely furnished, but flowers and indoor plants were abundant. D'Ayala could hear voices from behind closed doors, and there was a faint smell of cooking and disinfectant. Matron came into sight, approaching along a corridor where gleaming linoleum reflected her serviceable shoes, and she rustled with starch at every step, yet when she spoke her voice was soft Irish.

'So you'll be the Professor from Sicily who's come to see Dr Kaplan,' she said. 'He'll be glad you're here, poor soul. Friends are with him right now, but you can go straight in. It's that door there.'

'Thank you,' said D'Ayala. 'Please tell me, is he very ill?'
'Oh, he's had bad trouble with his heart, you know. But right now he's not too bad at all.' And away she went to her many responsibilities.

D'Ayala knocked at Kaplan's door gently. No answer came, but now he could hear voices and soft laughter. He knocked harder. The voices stopped and the door was opened by a dark man in a pin-striped suit.

'Excuse me, is this Dr Kaplan's room?'
'Yes, yes, please come in.' The man was almost obsequious.

D'Ayala entered the room with the hesitancy of an Englishman and felt at once amongst strangers. Kaplan lay in bed in one corner surrounded by friends, Jewish doctors and their wives, the men in sombre suits and the women in trouser suits and butcher-boy caps of sizzling colour, cheerful and un-English. They all looked at D'Ayala with kind smiles and curious eyes as they drew aside so that he could see Kaplan, small and fragile, propped against pillows in a metal hospital bed. Without a word Kaplan raised thin arms and held them out to D'Ayala in a gesture that made him think of the Bible. D'Ayala went forward at once, grasped Kaplan's hands, leaned over him, kissed his forehead, and stepped back from the bedside.

'Children,' said Kaplan, 'this is my friend, Lorenzo D'Ayala, from Palermo.' There were welcoming murmurs and hands reached out to shake D'Ayala's. Kaplan spoke again, this time to D'Ayala. 'Friends from Heidelberg and Vienna, friends from years and years. Ah, D'Ayala, how good it is to see you here.'

'You knew that I would come?'

'Of course. I was certain.'

But the group round the bed had begun to talk again, caught in the cross-currents of old friendships. Kaplan listened, smiling and secure. When D'Ayala leaned towards him to talk, he shrugged his shoulders in apology. At such moments, how can two share?

So D'Ayala sat back in a chair and tried to follow the talk all around him. After half a lifetime spent in England, there was nothing English about these people. They spoke the language in strong accents and strangely ordered phrases, but with great care as if they had agreed among themselves never to lapse into their own tongue. D'Ayala did not always find it easy to grasp their meaning, and he was confused by their lifestyle: these were aerial nomads journeying about the world, touching down in Israel to visit relations, in America to see grandchildren, in Vienna to stay with friends, and calling anywhere and everywhere that Jewish families had put down fragile roots. D'Ayala felt that nowhere, to them, was truly home.

His nearest neighbour was an elderly woman perched on the edge of Kaplan's bed, not far from his feet. She turned to Kaplan for a moment, leaning towards his face and patting his knee and said, 'Your poor friend here must feel lost among us Jews!'

'Now he knows what it's like to be a minority,' said Kaplan.

She turned to D'Ayala. 'It must be a long, long time since you saw George, Professor. What a pity you find him in bed here.'

And a pity, thought D'Ayala, to find him such an old man, as if he had jumped back one generation. He must be quite out of touch with modern times.

'Have you a family?' the woman on the bed was asking.

'Yes, I have a son.'

85

'A son is fine. I have a son, too, and a daughter at university.' She gave a full account of her children and their accomplishments. 'And so goodlooking you wouldn't believe,' she ended, her face pink with happiness. 'And George's son,' she said, turning to Kaplan to make sure he was listening, 'you've heard about George's son? Such a success that boy, a real businessman headed for the top.' She was smiling at Kaplan, trying to make amends for the son who had turned his back on his father's values and gone into the world of money-making for its own sake. If either of her children had done that, it would have broken her heart.

The door to Kaplan's room opened and a nurse came in with his lunch on a trolley. She approached the bed as his visitors moved aside. She then arranged his napkin for him under his chin and began talking to him as if he were a child.

'Here we are then, dear, a nice lunch. Fish again, that's your favourite, isn't it? With peas and mashed potatoes. Sit up a bit more, now. Can you reach properly? Try not to spill things. You must be tired, talking to all these nice friends.'

Kaplan wasn't listening to a word she said. He was trying to catch D'Ayala's eye, but there were too many flailing arms, too many umbrellas to be sorted out, too many voices speaking together, too much helpfulness and good wishes. D'Ayala was submerged in it all.

'Would you mind,' said Kaplan to the nurse, 'would you mind telling the gentleman from Sicily that I want a word with him.'

'In a minute, dear, in a minute. I want to get you all fixed up first.'

'But he's about to go.'

'Then I'd better fetch him. Now which one is he?'

Kaplan smiled. 'Just call out "Dottore" and you'll see,' he said.

But D'Ayala had heard them. He came to the bedside.

'Lorenzo, I have to rest after my food, and I haven't talked to you at all. Will you come back later? They bring tea at four o'clock. You should take it with me.'

'Of course,' said D'Ayala.

'I have important things to tell you,' said Kaplan.

'I'll be here,' said D'Ayala, and as he spoke one of the doctor friends came over and slipped a hand through his arm, saying, 'Come, I'll give you a lift back to town.'

Chapter 19

D'Ayala came back to the nursing home at teatime. Morning twilight had persisted all day, and Kaplan's room was shadowy except for a single pool of light cast on the bed. Kaplan lay on his back, as still and formal as a corpse, his eyes closed, his eyelids transparent blue, his cheeks caved in leaving his thin lips bonded together as if they had been glued.

'I'm too late,' thought D'Ayala, 'he hasn't long to go.' Kaplan's feebleness reminded D'Ayala that he himself had not yet experienced any of the common infirmities of old age except impotence, and even that might be illusory since he hadn't put it to the test. He was, in fact, indecently fit.

Suddenly Kaplan opened his eyes and looked at D'Ayala as intently as a bird. 'You thought I was asleep,' said Kaplan.

'And weren't you?'

'Not at all. I was eavesdropping on your mind. You were saying to yourself, "Kaplan is finished." But you were not quite right. I am still a social animal.'

'I noticed that this morning,' said D'Ayala.

'Ah, my surrogate family. They don't want me to feel alone with Miriam gone and my son so busy.'

'I remember your son. Bernard, isn't it? What does he do?'

'Diamonds,' said Kaplan. 'He makes money with diamonds. That's something I know nothing about. I wanted him to join the publishing business so that we could talk, but it was not to be.'

'You wanted him to be a Jewish intellectual,' said D'Ayala, smiling.

'I suppose so.' Kaplan smiled back, but only for a second. Then he became serious and said, 'He's embarrassed by what he calls the glamour of my generation, all victims and martyrs and heroes. He doesn't feel anything in common with them: in fact, he had quite an identity problem.' A wry smile crept across Kaplan's face. 'When you see him, look at the ring on his right hand. It's his initials all in diamonds.'

'Sons can be surprising,' said D'Ayala.

Kaplan paused to reflect. Then he said, 'Bernard didn't even want to keep any of the paintings. He kept saying I should sell them, and so I did.'

'The sale you mentioned in your letter to me?' asked D'Ayala.

'Yes. It was a month ago. To tell you the truth, I put it in my letter as a ruse to get you here. Have I annoyed you?'

'No, of course not. The irony of the matter is that in any case I couldn't have represented the Institute – or bid for anything myself – because I've been fired.'

'Fired?' Kaplan was incredulous. His voice wavered over the word as if he was not absolutely sure what it meant.

'Jettisoned. Thrown out of my post as archivist.' D'Ayala had intended to be brief, but instead heard himself lamenting not only his departure from the Institute but his shock at Mariella's death, his disappointment in Laura and Paolo, his anonymity in the eyes of his grandson, and even the departure of his maids. The spate of words ran away with him, everything came out in lumpish phrases and he felt as if, by mentioning his woes, he had brought them about. At last he finished.

'Oh Kaplan, I'm so sorry, I must have tired you. I didn't mean to talk like this. I don't know what came over me. I'll go now and let you rest. Is there anything I can do for you?'

'Yes, as a matter of fact there is. Do you remember my house in Wimbledon? It's been cleared now. Everything went to one saleroom or another except one painting. Would you go to the house and get it for me?'

'Certainly I will.'

'When you see it you'll remember it,' said Kaplan. 'It's the first painting I ever bought and you lent me the money. In San Gimignano. Do you remember?'

'As if it were yesterday. Ours is a long friendship.'

'And a good one,' added Kaplan. For a moment he was dreamy, but soon he rallied. 'You should take the painting to this address,' he said as his thin fingers scratched the top of the bedside table hunting for a scrap of paper. When he found it, he handed it to D'Ayala. On it was written in shaky capital letters an address in Kensington. 'Do you know where that is?'

'Edwards Square,' said D'Ayala, 'yes, I know where that is. My mother's cousin had a house there once, I believe.'

'This is a basement flat on the west side. A close friend of mine lives there. The painting will introduce you. It's very important to me that you should meet.' He lay back against the pillows, apparently exhausted. D'Ayala quietly left the room.

Chapter 20

At two o'clock next afternoon D'Ayala stood in the front garden of Kaplan's house in Wimbledon. A heavy yellow sky pressed down above; blowsy leaves, tired of summer, hung thick and damp from deciduous trees; elderly weeds had pierced the gravel on the drive and were sprawling, exhausted, underfoot. The house itself, a large white nineteen-thirties concoction, looked ghostly rather than crisply smart. D'Ayala approached the front door, inserted the key, found that the door opened with surprising ease as if to welcome him. He stepped inside and was at once assailed by the strong smell of an empty house and the sad creak of floorboards that had until recently been covered by carpets of uncalled for thickness and cost. He turned left, into the sitting-room.

'But it wasn't like this,' he said to himself. 'Never. I have never been here before.'

In uncertain memory, Kaplan's sitting-room had been beautiful. The room that D'Ayala now saw was not. It had no grace of proportion, no colour, no light. The windows were smeary and let in little of the yellowish day outside, floorboards were stained or split, and the whole room was broken up into mean little cells between bookstacks that reached, in parallel, from the back wall of the room to its centre, shelf after shelf lined with black dust where the books had been.

D'Ayala turned to the fireplace. It was hideous, covered in tiles the colour of porridge. Crumpled papers had been thrown into its black maw. Dreamily D'Ayala moved some of the paper with his foot, and there he found a half-burned log on a bed of ashes. The sight cleared his memory instantly. This was indeed the room he had known. Sparks had flown from the log as it was thrown on to the fire, and he saw their reflection in the well-polished tiles, he saw small ornaments set out on the mantelshelf, souvenirs from Israel and Egypt in glass, wood, stone, tiny statuettes in bronze, small jade bowls.

When he turned to the room he found the windows curtained and dressed with deep pelmets that improved their proportions, the floors carpeted, armchairs before the fire with arms and backs so wide that they invited one to lie rather than sit, and cushions of many colours, mostly hand embroidered. And from the middle of the room to the back wall reached the bookstacks with the real splendour of the room, books by the hundred bound in velvet, leather, card, paper, books in many languages from different periods and publishers, books on all kinds of topics. Strolling back and forth along those book stacks as D'Ayala had done years before, fantasy was fed: one could be, from one minute to the next, a philosopher, musician, water engineer, Rabbi, psychiatrist, breeder of sheep or horses or dahlias or microorganisms, captain of industry, inmate of Treblinka, tasting each role simply by opening a book and rejecting it by slapping the book shut.

On the back wall of the room, facing the fireplace between each pair of book stacks, hung a painting. Kaplan had acquired works by those closest to his heart: Klimt, Kokoschka, Schiele, Adler.

As in memory D'Ayala looked at them, Miriam came into the room and set down a silver tray with coffee cups on it.

'I still have a few things from my family,' she said, sitting down and leaning over the tray to pour. 'Just a few things.'

'They're beautiful,' said D'Ayala.

Suddenly Kaplan appeared, lounging back in one of the big chairs and offering D'Ayala a cigar. Then sound was added to the memory: a recording of a Schubert string quartet, and in one corner of the room D'Ayala remembered a violin case propped against a music stand. But when he had asked Kaplan if he played, the answer was vague. 'I need practice, one always needs practice. Sometimes I go and play with a friend.'

The scenario of memory was about to fade when D'Ayala heard sounds in the hall outside, the latch of the front door clicking as if someone had difficulty in opening it, then small thumps, then a heavy one. Miriam stood up looking pale. Kaplan was saying firmly, 'Go to bed Miriam, leave this to me.' There was some confusion of timing and events, but eventually D'Ayala remembered hearing a voice outside the door.

'Come along now, come along. You can't lie there. Come into the kitchen and I'll make you some coffee.' It was Kaplan speaking.

In answer there came a boy's voice, Bernard's. 'I don't want any bloody coffee. Leave me alone. I can take care of myself. Just get out of my way.'

Yes, that had been it. Bernard, aged fourteen, was an alcoholic. D'Ayala remembered Kaplan's apologies, Miriam's terrible anxiety, and how thankful he himself had been that Paolo had at least missed that trap. Later he understood that Bernard had been cured, but it had taken time and money and Miriam had suffered depression as a lasting result.

D'Ayala looked down at the fireplace again. The blackened log and crumpled papers were back, the present was here again.

Bernard's problem was past, and his present lifestyle could be tolerated amiably. Time heals all wounds. Or does it, wondered D'Ayala. Time had not improved his relationship with Paolo, rather the reverse. The unprepossessing boy had become the exasperating man, difficult to love, impossible to admire. He hoped that old age would make him more tolerant.

In the meantime, he pushed Paolo out of his mind and walked to the end of the room. Here were the windows and what light there was. And here, round the end of the last of the bookstacks, was a clear view of the San Gimignano Madonna still hanging on the back wall, lighting up her allotted space with colour and vivacity.

'You too are far from home,' D'Ayala said to her. 'And you've been here all these years but still look like a foreigner.'

The little Madonna was seated, but her chair was hidden by the voluminous folds of her blue silk gown. On her lap was the Christchild, more doll than human being, and held unconvincingly between her podgy girlish hands. It was her face that dominated the painting, a young face dimpled with a smile of satisfaction. She seemed to have come straight from the arms of the painter to sit for him yet again, establishing progressive entitlement to his house, food and fortune, as well as his bed.

As D'Ayala watched, her face faded and mixed into that of Alba. Her hands became Alba's hands, competent and useful. The doll-baby disappeared completely. Then it was difficult to see at all because he was weeping, and whispering 'Alba, Alba' through his tears.

Relieved by this catharsis, D'Ayala gathered clean newspapers from the floor, took down the painting and wrapped it up, and left. The house trembled from the crash of the front door closing in the empty hall.

Walking down the steep hill towards Wimbledon Station, D'Ayala did not notice the traffic or people who passed him. He carried the painting against his chest, held with both arms, clutched and nursed. He was trying to imagine the touch of human skin, that healer. He tried to remember his mother's touch on his baby body, but could not. He tried to remember the feel of her fingers on his sweaty forehead, wiping aside his hair when he was fifteen and she had beaten him yet again at tennis, but he could only visualise the gesture, not feel the sensation. He tried to recall Mariella's touch, but her hands had been dull and unimaginative and left no lingering memory of a caress. He did remember, with stern pride, that he had never once touched Alba. He recalled, with shame, that he had once read an article in a newspaper about Americans who met to touch each other, strangers though they were, and that the idea had disgusted him. His yearning was now so strong that he could only believe them to have been right.

From Wimbledon station he took a near-empty train to Kensington High Street, and there walked out to crowded pavements where young Arabs thrust political pamphlets at him, tourists wandered uncertainly outside the shops, and elderly women waited for buses under the rain against a background of nervy, noisy traffic.

D'Ayala wondered who could direct him. He bought a newspaper and put it on his head to keep off the rain, and asked the vendor.

'Edwards Square, guv? Past the Odeon cinema turn left.'

Chapter 21

Harriet Fielding arrived at her basement flat in Edwards Square feeling tired out and miserable. She had been with Kaplan since early morning, but he had been comatose, only occasionally roused for a few minutes, and then able to say very little. Sitting there, watching him helplessly, she thought that many people would pray. But what sort of prayer could she offer? 'Oh God, please let him live on and on because I need him and I am only thirty-seven?' The request was not likely to be granted. At the pit of her stomach were chill and nausea and she was angry with herself for succumbing to them. Hadn't she prepared herself for this situation, reminding herself over and over again that young women are bound to lose elderly lovers, and trying to believe that by facing this simple truth she would be armed and ready for the event? 'When it comes,' she admitted, 'one is helpless as a baby. There's no defence.'

She went down the steps to the door of the flat and stopped to find her key, balancing her briefcase on a raised knee while a heavy plastic bag of groceries pulled at her wrist and her hair fell forward over her face. Eventually she discovered the key in the pocket of her blazer.

Once inside the flat, she went straight to the sitting-room and flopped down on the chesterfield, letting the briefcase and grocery bag slide down to her feet. At least she had not found Lorenzo D'Ayala waiting for her on the doorstep. Kaplan had managed to tell her that D'Ayala had arrived in London at last, and would come to see her later in the day.

Kaplan was obsessed with D'Ayala. Ever since he had received D'Ayala's letter from Palermo he had been painting a portrait of the man in Harriet's mind with memories, facts, impressions, all of them positive, most of them flattering. 'You'll like him, I know you will. He'll be a good friend to you just as he has been to me. I shan't be leaving you entirely alone once you've met D'Ayala. And he will come, you'll see.'

But now that she was to meet D'Ayala in flesh and blood, with the perversity of human nature she had begun to wish that he would not come, would not complicate her feelings, would not stir those of Kaplan who so needed serenity. She even resented the practical effort D'Ayala was bound to cause her simply because he was an elderly foreigner accustomed to comfort and service and here in London with no social contacts other than herself. He was bound to be demanding, and she was drained.

She got to her feet, leaving the briefcase on the floor but dragging the carrier bag of groceries behind her. She would go and get tea ready.

In the kitchen she dumped the bag on the table and looked around. The kitchen was too efficient to be welcoming and, as in most houses, a warm bolthole. She climbed on to a stool to reach the top shelf of a cupboard that had been built right up to the ceiling, clutched at shelves for support, and took out a green baize bag that she hadn't touched for months. When she got down again she took from the bag a silver teapot in need of cleaning. A rub on her sleeves was all it got.

She thought of the day years ago when Kaplan had first seen that teapot.

'What a fine talisman!' he had said.

'Talisman?'

'Of course. I can see your past in every curve of it. Plenty of money and security. Was it your mother's?'

'Yes.'

'And now you need it for reassurance. When you see it you

can be certain that nothing has really changed in your world. Don't I read you like a book?' They had laughed like conspirators.

But today there was no reassurance from the sight of the silver teapot. Harriet stood it on a tray with two cups. She heard the front door bell ring and went to answer it.

Lorenzo D'Ayala stood at the door with his shoulders hunched, his collar turned up, and a questioning look on his face. From under the breast of his coat protruded the Madonna in her newspaper wrappings.

'Have I come to the right address?' he asked.

'You must be Doctor D'Ayala. Do come in, it's awfully wet.'

D'Ayala stepped into the hall.

'I should introduce myself – I'm Harriet Fielding.'

D'Ayala heard, in the inflections of the voice, his mother. And looking at this English woman he was strongly reminded of her. Harriet Fielding was tall and spare, with long, narrow feet and hands and muted sex appeal. She was wearing, at that moment, an expression of deep weariness. Apparently she began to feel self-conscious under his open, Italian stare, for she lowered her eyes and smoothed back her hair. D'Ayala remembered his mother's hair, worn in coils like snail shells over her ears. She had called them 'earphones'.

D'Ayala was struggling to shed his coat without dropping the Madonna.

'Oh, I'm sorry, do let me help you,' said Harriet when she realised his difficulty. 'There. Now let's go into the sitting-room.'

As he followed her, D'Ayala looked down and was displeased with his muddy shoes and the crease of his trousers that had almost disappeared.

'I'm sorry this room is in such a mess,' she was saying as she picked up the briefcase and some books from the floor. D'Ayala, looking round, found the room warm, shabby and cosy as a womb. A Victorian desk piled with papers stood in one corner, a cello in a battered case in another. Shelves of books rose from floor to ceiling and in front of the chesterfield a gas fire was burning.

D'Ayala sank into the chesterfield's tired springs and his

knees stuck up like a grasshopper's. Carefully he laid the madonna in her damp wrappings down beside him. He felt bold enough to hold the palms of his hands out to the fire.

'You were expecting me,' he said.

Harriet, sitting on a stool nursing her knees, said, 'Well, yes, I must admit that I was.'

'George Kaplan asked me to come.'

'I know.' She wondered how much D'Ayala knew or guessed about this encounter and felt that he deserved some explanation. 'I think I ought to tell you that Kaplan has talked about you a great deal. He's told me how you met and about your family in Palermo and your adventures exploring Sicily together and about Vienna and the music and about your studies and the marvellous things you know about paintings and history and how interesting you make them. He told me about the war years, too, and the times when he thought he had lost contact with you and then discovered that you had both survived. He told me about your visits to London since then, and how it was always the same, your friendship, a warm constancy that he felt over any distance or time.'

'He was right,' said D'Ayala. 'But you must be fed up with me by now!' He was laughing.

'No, I have a special soft spot for your generation – and its reminiscences,' said Harriet, and she smiled at last. Looking at D'Ayala she found him just as beautiful as Kaplan had said, and she was glad that he was there. She wondered how shocked he would be if he knew the plans that Kaplan had for the two of them. 'In any case, it was your letter that inspired him,' she said.

'Inspired him?'

'Yes. With . . . new ideas, new hope. He longed to see you again before it was too late.'

D'Ayala seemed satisfied with her explanation. 'By the way,' he said, 'he asked me to bring you this.' The madonna in her humble wrappings was handed over.

Harriet opened the parcel on her knee, unfolding the newspaper carefully layer by layer until at last the painting lay revealed in her lap. 'It's the Madonna from the Wimbledon house,' she said. 'I saw it there just once. It's lovely.' She picked the painting up and held it out in front of her at arm's length, smiling and thinking to herself that this must surely be the most beautiful gift tag in the whole world and who would have thought of giving it to her with D'Ayala but Kaplan?

D'Ayala, watching her, wondered about her relationship with his friend. The painting was a handsome gift, and must have special meaning. 'I think you've known Kaplan for a long time,' he said.

'Oh yes, for years. When you saw him in the nursing home, didn't he tell you about me?' she asked hesitantly.

'Of course he did, yes, of course,' said D'Ayala, hoping that she would believe him.

She stood up and put the Madonna on the mantelpiece. 'There. She can survey the whole room from that position. It's so like Kaplan to remember that I loved her as soon as I saw her,' she said. 'And now I think we should have some tea.'

D'Ayala followed Harriet to the kitchen and was surprised to find it as modern and well-equipped as the one in Milan. 'Kaplan had the kitchen done,' said Harriet, 'but it still feels strange to me. I'm not at home with it. But wasn't it a lovely present?'

'Magnificent,' said D'Ayala. As she poured boiling water into the pot, he saw Alba in the Palermo kitchen upending the coffee pot with aplomb and wiping her hands on the seat of her stiff new jeans. Yet it was Harriet who was talking. What was she saying?

'Some cake? Will you have some cake?'

He pulled himself sharply into the present. 'Thank you, that would be excellent,' he said.

Harriet picked up the teatray and together they went back to the sitting-room.

'My mother used to make tea in Palermo,' said D'Ayala, 'and I wouldn't touch it. I thought it was medicine!'

'Kaplan told me a lot about your parents. Especially your mother.' They smiled at each other, both pleased, and for a time they sat back watching the fire in silence. Eventually Harriet moved.

'This flat is full of apprehension,' she said. 'I feel it as soon as I sit still. Every corner seems to know about Kaplan and to be waiting. Do you think rooms absorb emotions from the people who live in them?'

'It's possible,' said D'Ayala, remembering the sensations he had felt when he opened Mariella's work chest. 'And Kaplan must have been very happy here.'

'Oh, he was. It's unbelievable that he'll never set foot in these rooms again. I just can't take it in. I think that's why he wants you to stay, at least for a while.'

'To stay here?'

'Would you mind? The chesterfield makes a good bed.'

'If you're quite sure – but what about my things at the hotel?'

'Can you manage without them until tomorrow? I must go back to Kaplan this evening.'

They lapsed into silence again, but not for long. The telephone rang and Harriet answered it.

'Yes, yes, I'll come at once. Thank you for ringing me.' She put the receiver down.

'It was the nursing home,' said D'Ayala.

'Yes. He's taken a sudden turn for the worse. I must go. Will you wait for me here?'

'Of course. And while you're gone I ought to write an important letter.'

'There's everything in my desk over there – just help yourself,' she said. 'There's some whisky, too, on the kitchen sideboard.' She was already putting on her raincoat and a moment later she had left the flat.

D'Ayala, sitting alone, was less upset by the news of Kaplan's sudden deterioration than by a sense of guilt. He had neglected Paolo and Laura. He had not even told them of his safe arrival.

In Harriet's desk he found paper and envelopes, and he sat by the fireside wondering what to write. It was not until he deliberately visualised Paolo sitting beside him that he was able to think clearly. He wrote:

> My dear children,
> I am writing to tell you that I am well, in every sense, and you must no longer worry about me. Changes are

taking place in my mind and spirits, changes deeper than you would imagine. I am beginning to see my age from a new viewpoint – it excuses me from conventional duties and roles and leaves me free to start afresh. I have decided to stay here for the foreseeable future, so you should dispose of my belongings in any way you please.

I shall need a small allowance to live on, but that should not be difficult to arrange.

I hold you both always in my warmest affection.

Lorenzo D'Ayala

He put the letter into an envelope and sealed it at once before he could have any doubts or loss of courage. Then he lay back on the chesterfield and relaxed.

Around him the room was already getting dark after the murky day. Shadows blurred the outlines of furniture, colours turned to shades of grey, and the gas fire seemed to brighten minute by minute, illuminating the hearth and fender and the little Madonna who now glowed in her place on the mantelpiece as she, too, kept vigil.

In the far corner of the room D'Ayala noticed again the cello leaning up against the bookshelves. Idly he imagined Harriet opening the case, taking out the instrument, sitting down, tuning and preparing to play. She was not, however, alone. Near her sat Kaplan, settling his violin under his chin, Kaplan in good health, with the violin from the house in Wimbledon. Now Harriet leaned forward, surrounding the cello in an embrace, her fingers holding the fingerboard close to her cheek, her right hand stroking one string with her bow, the cello giving a deep note of pure pleasure.

The image began to change. Slowly the cello became Kaplan in Harriet's embrace, his short body against her long one, his face where the fingerboard had been, his eyes closed. He was wearing a smile of delight.

Oh, Kaplan, what a lucky man you have been! Oh, Harriet, let me feel your talents! I long for them, whispered D'Ayala in his mind.

He felt no regrets and no fear of failure and he took no backward glances at Alba.

Hunger of a different kind now seized him. Up he got and made for the kitchen. Just as she had promised, Harriet had left a bottle of whisky on the sideboard and he helped himself generously. The teatray was still on the table, so he cut himself a thick hunk of cake. It had been passable with the tea: now it tasted like ambrosia. He ate another piece, and all the crumbs he could collect. Then, feeling very much better, he went back to his place by the fire.

As he sat there he began to contemplate Kaplan's approach to death, the creeping journey through hours and minutes to the final beat when all would be achieved. D'Ayala felt privileged in being allowed, mentally and spiritually, to accompany Kaplan towards this goal, and in being able, through memories, to preserve Kaplan's dignity. D'Ayala's parents and wife had all died so suddenly that there had been no chance to prepare or to adjust perspectives. By contrast, Kaplan's dying was seemly.

After it would come the birth of a new world, a world without Kaplan but perhaps with a new beginning, a new beginning, if D'Ayala dared to imagine it, with Harriet. Dreaming thus, he fell asleep.

The sound of a car pulling up in the street outside woke him and a moment later the front door opened and Harriet came into the room.

'How is he?' asked D'Ayala.

'He's going. I don't think we shall see him again.'

'May I get you a drink?'

She sipped some whisky, sitting beside D'Ayala, staring at the fire.

'He had another attack this afternoon, and didn't know me at all this evening.' Tears trickled slowly down her cheeks.

'I'm sure he knew you were there,' said D'Ayala.

'The nurses said so. All the same, they made me come home. To rest, they said, just for a while. I suppose they had sent for Bernard.' She sniffed and D'Ayala gave her his handkerchief. There seemed nothing more to say.

At last the telephone rang. Harriet crossed the room, picked up the receiver and crouched over it, shivering. She listened and mumbled acknowledgement. Slowly she put the receiver down.

'He's gone,' she said. 'Ten minutes ago.'

As she came back across the room to the fireside, her arms rose towards D'Ayala and he stood waiting for her. When she reached him, she put her arms round his neck and drew him towards her and began to sway back and forth.

'Come,' said D'Ayala, 'come with me.'

He did not dislodge her arms, but turned sideways within their circle so that he stood by her side. Then he put his arm round her waist and urged her gently, very gently, towards her bed.